T[illegible]
Raven's
Shadow

James E. Wisher

JAMES E. WISHER

James E. Wisher

The Aegis of Merlin:

The Impossible Wizard

The Awakening

The Chimera Jar

The Raven's Shadow

Edited by: Janie Linn Dullard

Cover Art by: Paganus

Sand Hill Publishing 410171.0

ISBN 13: 978-1-945763-13-7

Chapter 1

Heading Home

Conryu yawned, snuggled deeper into his soft chair, and glanced out the window. The train was pulling into Central Station. In the distance the black Department building drew his eye. Despite being only half as tall as some of the surrounding skyscrapers it still managed to dominate the skyline. It was probably the aura of the unnatural that surrounded it. Either that or the presence of Kelsie's grandmother inside twisted reality.

Speaking of which, he'd offered to let Kelsie ride with them, but she'd insisted on staying in her private cabin. She claimed to be tired, but Conryu suspected she felt like a third wheel when Maria was around. He really hoped the two girls eventually learned to get along. He was very fond of both of them and it would make his life a lot easier if they liked each other at least a little.

Across from him Maria had her nose buried in one of the books she'd brought home with her. Why on earth she'd want to do more studying after all they'd done at school this past year baffled him. The only reason he'd brought Prime was because he had no choice. A powerful bond connected him to the scholomantic. If they were separated by more than a hundred or so yards the results would be painful for them both.

The brakes whined as the train slowed and came to a stop. The majority of the students would disembark here before boarding trains to other parts of the Alliance. Conryu and Maria had the good fortune—at least, good fortune in terms of avoiding potential assassins—not to have to leave their cabin. The whole car would be added to the train headed for Sentinel City.

Maria looked up from her book. "Are we there?"

"We're at the capital, but we've still got a long way to go."

"Oh." She lowered her face back to the book and was instantly lost in her own world.

Conryu shook his head and smiled. Must be nice.

Of course, Prime would like nothing better than to spend every moment cramming his head full of new spells. Conryu was a good deal less enthusiastic about studying, preferring to learn what he needed when he needed it. His hope was that he wouldn't need any magic this summer.

In the hall outside, a door slammed and a moment later a muffled voice protested.

Maria looked up again. "What was that?"

"Beats me." Conryu strode over and opened the door.

A big guy in a black suit had Kelsie by the wrist and was dragging her toward the exit. A second man had her bags.

"Hey!" All three turned to look at him. "What the hell are you two doing?"

The man with the bags scowled through his goatee. "Ms. Kincade is coming home with us. Return to your cabin and there won't be any trouble."

"You think you can kidnap my friend and there won't be any trouble?" He stepped out into the hall. "Let her go and get lost. Then there won't be any trouble."

"Conryu, these are my mom's private security guards. If she told them to bring me home they won't let me go."

"Do you want to go with them?"

"No."

He glared at the men in black through narrowed eyes. "Then we have a problem."

The nearest man tossed Kelsie's bags to the ground and reached under his coat. When Conryu saw the pistol he threw his hand forward. "Shatter!"

The gun burst into a handful of metal filings. In the guard's moment of surprise Conryu stepped in with a snap kick to the side of his knee.

When the guard's knee hit the hall floor Conryu spun into a slashing elbow to his opponent's temple. The guard's head thumped off the wall and he collapsed in a heap.

The second guard appeared uncertain whether he should release Kelsie and fight or try and drag her out of the train car. Conryu stepped over the unconscious figure and advanced down the hall.

The still-standing guard thrust Kelsie in front of him. "Don't come any closer."

"Or what? You expect me to believe you might hurt your employer's daughter?" Conryu concentrated on Kelsie. "Cloak of Darkness!"

Liquid black covered Kelsie from head to toe.

"Gah!" The guard thrust her away from him. He clearly had no idea what the spell did, just as Conryu had hoped.

Conryu pulled Kelsie behind him. Maria stood in the doorway and held out her hand. "Come on."

Kelsie hesitated for just a moment before ducking into the cabin. Maria nodded to him, slammed the door shut and snapped the lock.

Conryu stared at the still-conscious guard. "Just you and me now. If you want to leave I promise I won't tell anyone."

The guard fell into a fighting stance. "You took Freddy by surprise. I won't go down so easy."

"Did you see what I did to his gun? I could do that to your head just as easily."

The guard's Adam's apple bobbed as sweat poured down his face. Conryu didn't actually know if such a simple spell would blast the guard's head to bits, though it stood to reason the spell affected living flesh as well as it did nonliving material. The truth was even if it did work that way, he wouldn't do it, but Freddy's pal didn't know that.

The guard lowered his fists. "You don't understand. If we go back without Lady Kincade's daughter she'll fire us at best."

Conryu didn't have much sympathy for men who would kidnap a girl just because their employer told them to. "Try to look on the bright side. At least you'll still be alive to search for a new job."

He stepped back over Freddy, who was now groaning on the floor, and stood beside his cabin door. Conryu raised his hand. "Take him and go. Last warning."

"Alright, alright. Just so you know, I'm blaming you for all this." The guard collected his partner and the pair of them stumbled off the train.

Conryu sighed and lowered his hand. They'd bought his bluff. Thank goodness.

* * *

Conryu waited until the two goons were off the train before he turned and knocked. "They're gone, let me in."

A second later the lock clicked open and he slid the door aside. Maria returned to her seat across from Kelsie, who was still covered in his Cloak of Darkness spell. Conryu waved his hand and the darkness vanished.

The guard's tight grip had raised a set of nasty bruises on Kelsie's wrist. "You okay?" he asked.

"Yeah, but Mom's going to be really mad. I mean, I knew she wasn't going to be happy I ignored her order, but I never thought she'd send two of her personal bodyguards to drag me home."

"Let me see your arm." Maria gently took Kelsie's bruised wrist in her hand. She chanted a spell and a bright glow surrounded her hand. She rubbed the injuries and Kelsie sighed.

"You know," Maria said. "I wasn't thrilled when Conryu invited you to come for a visit, but if this is how your family treats you I'm starting to think he should have offered to let you stay longer. There."

The glow disappeared revealing smooth, healed skin.

"Thank you." Kelsie lunged across the little table and hugged Maria. "For everything."

Conryu grinned and went back out to collect Kelsie's bags. He'd have to thank Kelsie's mother. Her thugs' attack had done more to make Maria sympathetic to her problems than anything he could have said. Maybe, just maybe, the two of them would start getting along better now.

He brought the bags inside and set them in the corner. There wasn't room enough in the overhead storage for two more suitcases. There also weren't enough chairs for all of them. He shrugged and sat on the floor, using her bags as a backrest.

"I'm sorry." Kelsie started to get up. "I'm taking your chair."

"Don't worry about it." He waved her back into the seat. "I doubt Dumb and Ugly will be back, but I'll feel better if I know where you are."

"I heard you talking through the door." Kelsie sat back down. "Would you have really killed that guy?"

"Naw. I'm not even sure if Shatter will work on living flesh."

In the storage area Conryu's bag shifted and bounced. He sighed, stood up, and unzipped it. A t-shirt flew out and zoomed around the cabin like a cheap Halloween ghost. Prime's muffled voice was unintelligible.

"Hold still." Prime hovered over the table and Conryu pulled the shirt off him. "What did you want?"

"I eavesdropped on your conversation and since it is my duty to educate you I attempted to escape and do so. Shatter isn't an effective spell for killing. That said, it's a simple thing for a powerful dark wizard to kill. All you need to do is focus on your target and say 'die' in Infernal."

"That sounds way too easy," Conryu said.

"The spell is simple, making it work is hard. You have to genuinely want the spell's target to die with all your will. The least bit of doubt and the spell will fail. I hesitate to find fault, Master, but I fear you lack the capacity to kill with magic. You're too kind hearted."

Maria shook her head. "That's not a fault. If Conryu could casually kill someone he wouldn't be who he is."

The cabin fell silent for half a minute before Kelsie asked, "So how long to reach Sentinel City?"

The mood lightened at once and Conryu settled back on his makeshift couch. He really didn't want to kill anyone, but as a warrior he knew enough to realize the day would come when he'd have to make a choice. He wouldn't always be able to win while leaving his enemies alive.

"Four or five hours on the train, plus however long it takes to drive to our building." Maria reached for her bag. "I have extra books if you'd like something to read."

"No, thank you. I don't think I could concentrate. I'm just going to rest my eyes and try to take a nap."

That sounded like an excellent idea, but Conryu was too keyed up to sleep. After half an hour or so the train got underway again. When they moved out of sight of Central City he finally allowed himself to relax.

Sometime later the train jerked. Conryu's eyes popped open and he was halfway to his feet before he noticed the station out the window. He must have dozed off after all. He twisted his neck from side to side to work the stiffness out.

Kelsie was softly snoring and he hated to wake her, but he didn't have enough hands to carry her and the bags. He gave her shoulder a shake and she groaned.

"Come on, wake up. We're here."

She blinked and sat up straight. Maria held out a napkin and tapped her chin. Kelsie wiped the drool off while turning beet red. She crumpled up the napkin and climbed out of her chair while Conryu collected his and Maria's bags.

"Think your parents will be here?" Conryu asked.

Maria shrugged and opened the door. "No idea. I can't get a straight answer whenever I ask about what's happening. I can tell Dad's stressed to the max and it's rubbing off on Mom. I hope at least one of them's here, but I'm not holding my breath."

"At least your parents aren't going to send someone to try and kidnap you," Kelsie said.

Maria laughed. "True, but not sending kidnappers is a pretty low bar. From what Conryu's told me I wouldn't trade parents with you for the world."

They made their way to the car door and climbed down to the platform. Since they were in the last cabin in the last car everyone had already disembarked and was making their way toward the lobby. The trio followed along at an easy pace.

"Think we can coax Mom into taking us to Giovanni's for dinner?" Conryu adjusted his grip on Maria's bag.

"I don't know, but that's an excellent plan. When's Jonny getting in?"

"I'm pretty sure he said the day after tomorrow."

"Who's Jonny?" Kelsie asked.

"Another old friend." Conryu grinned. "He's attending military school. His plan is to be deployed to Florida and defend scantily clad beach babes from zombies."

"That doesn't sound very likely." Kelsie glanced back at him. "He knows that, right?"

"He should, I've told him often enough. Jonny—"

"Conryu Koda!" Running down the platform was Kat Gable and her unlucky cameraman, Joe.

"Oh, for Christ's sake. Can't I get off the train just once without that lunatic waiting for me?"

Kelsie turned to face him. "You know Kat?"

"Sort of; she's my personal stalker. The woman is incapable of taking no for an answer."

"Do you know her?" Maria asked.

"Sure, she's interviewed me and my mom half a dozen times. Kat handles all the magic-related interviews for her network. She's tough, but fair, though one time my mom threatened to buy her station and fire her."

Kat reached them and thrust her microphone in Conryu's face. "How did you enjoy your first year at the Arcane Academy?"

Conryu glared into the camera. *Shatter!* The lens cracked and sparks shot out the back.

"Fuck me!" Joe dropped the camera and danced away a second before it burst into flames.

Conryu turned his gaze on Kat. "No comment."

She lowered the microphone and frowned. "How long are we going to have to play this game? Why don't you just give me the interview and we can both move on."

"If you want it to be over all you need to do is stop showing up wherever I am. I don't owe you a thing."

Kat shook her head then her eyes went wide. "Kelsie Kincade? I didn't even notice you there. What brings you to Sentinel City?"

"Visiting friends. Nice to see you again, Kat."

"We need to go. I imagine my mom's getting impatient." Conryu stalked past the now-silent Kat.

"Bye." Kelsie waved to the reporter and fell in behind him with Maria bringing up the rear.

When they were outside of Kat's range of hearing Maria said, "Did you make his camera explode?"

Conryu offered his best innocent look. "Me?"

"Yeah, you."

"Did I cast a spell?"

"No."

"There you go."

They left the platform and after a quick search through the many hugging families spotted Conryu's mom standing near one of the pillars on the right side of the entry area. She saw them at the same moment and waved before running over and hugging him.

After half a minute and several kisses Conryu wiggled free. "Hey, Mom. Dad waiting in the car?"

"Of course." Mom turned her attention to Kelsie. "Aren't you going to introduce me?"

"Sorry. Mom meet Kelsie Kincade. Kelsie, my mom."

They shook hands and Kelsie said, "Thanks so much for letting me stay with you. I hope I won't be too much of a bother."

"Not at all, dear. Sho and I are always glad to meet a friend of Conryu's. And such a famous one. I'm afraid you'll find our little apartment smaller than you're used to."

Kelsie smiled. "At school I share a room with eleven other girls, so rooming with three people won't be a problem."

"Did my parents not come?" Maria's disappointment came through loud and clear.

"No, Orin asked me to give you a ride home. Your mom was called out of the city on an emergency consultation and he's been working crazy hours at the Department. I have no idea what's happening, but everyone's nerves are stretched tight."

Maria slumped and Conryu wanted to give her a hug, but his hands were overloaded as it was. He couldn't have been more pleased when Kelsie did it for him. Even better, Maria didn't shrug her off. Summer was looking to be a good deal more pleasant than he'd first feared.

* * *

Kelsie screamed when Conryu opened the throttle on his bike and they roared down the highway. She'd never ridden on a motorcycle before, her mother said they were too dangerous. As she clutched Conryu's chest and watched the cars whiz by she thought she might have finally found something she and her mother agreed on.

What Kelsie couldn't deny was the thrill of it. Her heart raced and tears streamed down her face both from the wind and the excitement. It also provided an excellent excuse to hug Conryu which was something she'd never pass up.

He shot past a bus and she tightened her grip. When he'd shown her the gleaming black bike this morning she never imagined flying down the road at ninety miles an hour, her hair snapping behind her in the wind.

Last night had been her first experience sleeping on a couch and it was much nicer than she'd expected. Conryu's mother had fixed it up like a proper bed with soft sheets and a warm, snuggly blanket. She'd been so sweet, doing everything short of tucking Kelsie in to make her feel at home.

Kelsie couldn't help contrasting the welcome she'd received from these total strangers with the one her family gave her whenever she came home after a trip. Generally all she got was a combination of complaints and indifference. She'd been tempted to ask Mrs. Koda to adopt her on the spot and after the incident on the train that might still be an option. If nothing else she now understood why he said he wouldn't trade families with her for all the money in the world.

Conryu slewed the bike into the right lane, slowed, and pulled onto the off-ramp. They hadn't really had a destination, the trip was just an excuse for him to take his beloved bike for a spin.

After his parents and Maria, Kelsie was pretty sure Conryu loved his bike the most. When he'd uncovered it this morning he whispered to it and stroked it in a way that made her jealous. Kelsie would have loved to woken up that way. With his parents in the kitchen and Maria four floors up that didn't seem likely.

He wove through crowded city streets, to where, she couldn't say. Ten minutes later he pulled into a dirt lot. In the nearby park workers were building a fence around the perimeter. Conryu switched off the motor, put down the kickstand, and pulled off his helmet.

She copied him and shook out her hair, trying to restore some semblance of order. "What is this place?"

"This is the site of the annual Shadow Carnival. It's also where I was almost murdered for the second time. I'm not entirely sure why I came back here. It was like something drew me."

The flap on his saddlebag rustled and Prime flew out. She'd been so excited by the ride she'd forgotten all about the book.

"It's not unusual for the site of past trauma to haunt a person for years afterward. Don't be concerned, Master, there's nothing wrong with your mind."

"As always, Prime, you're a great comfort."

"So what happened here?" She'd never heard the whole story about Conryu's many brushes with death even though she'd lived through one of them.

When he finished telling her she shook her head. "So that's why you were curious about shadow beasts in our first class. I admit I was wondering."

"Why didn't you ask?"

"I was wary of you right up until my desperation got the best of me. Looking back, I can't believe how many weeks I wasted. If I'd just taken a chance that first day when you talked to me we could have become friends so much sooner."

"We're friends now, that's what counts." He patted her knee.

His gaze shifted to the sky. Hanging above them was the huge floating island. She'd seen this one before, though it didn't fly directly over Central. It looked like it was headed right for them, sort of a slow motion meteor from a movie.

"When's the carnival?" Kelsie asked.

"This weekend, when the island is directly overhead. It'll be so dark you'll think it's night at noon."

"Can we go?"

"I don't know if they'll let me in after what happened last year, but we can try. Maria and I have been going since we were little so it's a tradition and Jonny would never pass up a chance at junk food."

"How long have you known him?" Conryu had mentioned they were friends, but she didn't know anything else about him.

"Since third grade. He arrives from military school tomorrow for a one-month break." Conryu sighed. "And I thought we got screwed on vacation time. So what do you want to do after lunch?"

She shrugged. Kelsie was happy to do anything as long as it was with him.

* * *

Lady Raven stood on the small balcony of her redoubt and watched the island creep across the sky. It wouldn't be long now. After a year of sitting on her hands, hiding, and making preparations, at last everything would come together. And not a moment too soon as far as she was concerned. Another month cooped up with nothing but undead for company and she feared she might go mad.

Her black silk robe swirled around her as a warm summer breeze caressed her skin and carried the salty scent of the nearby ocean to her. The blue-green water lay on the opposite side of the building from where she stood. Lady Raven imagined it, the waves, the birds. The mental exercise soothed her for a few seconds before the blast of a ship's horn jolted her out of her reverie.

Just as well, really. The final meeting with the Hierarchs was due to begin in ten minutes. She needed to go back inside and prepare. Three steps carried her through the French doors and into her bedroom where two of the undead bikers she'd taken as her personal bodyguards stood against the wall waiting for orders. She'd left three of the others to guard the entrance to her base and the last was destroyed by Terra and her flunkies.

She brushed past her bed, pausing long enough to collect the black raven mask from her nightstand. On her way out she paused to look at herself in the dressing room mirror. Still old, still wrinkled, but still alive and more powerful than ever. That was an exchange the younger members of the Society wouldn't understand for many more years.

Satisfied, Lady Raven opened the door and stepped out into the hall. It was a short walk from the bedroom to her casting chamber, intentionally so, as she had to be available day or night for her superiors, especially now that the culmination of their work was so close at hand. Her guards fell in behind automatically.

There was no danger to her here and it seemed foolish to have the lumbering things following her everywhere, but better safe than sorry. The only rule was they weren't allowed in her casting chamber. The nature of their dark magic messed with her spells in unpredictable ways, so they stood guard outside while she stepped into the Spartan chamber.

When she first arrived she'd taken the time to inscribe a permanent spell circle in the floor, thus freeing herself from having to draw it again and again. The mask slipped over her head and settled into its familiar place. When this mission ended she'd miss the raven mask, but Hierarchs all wore animal masks;

only Sub-Hierarchs wore birds. It was an upgrade she was eager to make.

Once inside the circle she cleared her mind and prepared for her superiors to make contact. Five minutes later a faint tingle was followed by the appearance of the Hierarchs and Lady Bluejay. Of the horrid Lady Mockingbird there was no sign.

"All is in readiness?" Lady Dragon asked.

"Yes, Mistress. There has been no activity near the new hiding places and I've seen no activity at the Department that concerns me."

"Excellent. Tomorrow we release our demands. The weak men will do what we require or see the streets of their city choked with the dead."

"As you say, Lady Dragon." Lady Raven's eyes flicked to the spot usually occupied by her rival.

Lady Dragon didn't miss the minute gesture, precisely as she'd hoped. "Lady Mockingbird is dead."

The blunt admission set her on her heels for a moment. Had she so badly failed the Hierarchs that they felt the need to eliminate her?

"No, we didn't kill her." Lady Dragon leaned back in an unseen chair. "Her attempt to slay the abomination failed and her cover was pierced. She fell in battle with the head of dark magic, Angeline Umbra."

"A worthy foe. Pity about Lady Mockingbird."

Lady Dragon's laugh filled the space. "Spare us your false concern. The hatred between the two of you was well known. To pretend otherwise is an insult to all of us."

Lady Raven bowed her head. "I meant no offense. But I do have a suggestion."

"We will hear it," Lady Dragon said.

"What if we included turning over the abomination to us as part of our plans? We could let the fools in the Department do our work for us. That would be a small thing compared to releasing our leader."

Lady Dragon's mask covered her whole face, hiding her expression, but from the way she leaned forward Lady Raven hoped her idea had been well received.

"An excellent idea. It will be a simple matter to add it with potentially great gains. You will make a fine Hierarch, Lady Raven."

Her heart raced upon hearing Lady Dragon's compliment. She had never shown such open favoritism before.

"Be ready." Lady Dragon's figure started to fade away. "When the time comes it will be your responsibility to punish the city should their leaders fail to do as we require."

A second later Lady Raven was alone. None of the others had made so much as a sound. She didn't know what to make of it. Were they distancing themselves in case she failed or had Lady Dragon given orders for them to remain silent?

There was no way for her to know and that fact frightened her almost as much as the completion of her mission excited her. In a few days her fate would be sealed one way or the other.

Chapter 2

Ultimatum

"Long time no see, bro!" Jonny stepped through the door and bumped fists with Conryu.

In the ten months since Conryu'd last seen his second-oldest friend, Jonny had traded his ripped jeans for fatigues, gotten a military-spec buzz cut, and put on about ten pounds of muscle. His already bronze skin had darkened and unless Conryu was mistaken he'd gotten a new scar on his right arm.

"Looks like the army agrees with you." Conryu motioned him to the couch and shut the door.

Jonny managed two steps before he froze. Kelsie was sitting on the couch with a slightly nervous smile. She had on a scoop-neck red dress that hugged her curves in a way that would annoy Maria when she arrived with the food.

Conryu smacked his forehead with his palm. He'd forgotten to mention Kelsie would be visiting in his last letter.

"Who's the babe and does Maria know she's here?" Jonny couldn't stop looking, not that Conryu blamed him.

"Jonny Salazar meet Kelsie Kincade. Kelsie, this is Jonny." They shook hands and Conryu gave his friend a playful shove toward the recliner before sitting beside Kelsie. "So how was your first year?"

"Boring. Dude, you wouldn't believe it. Every day, marching, calisthenics, shooting, and more marching. On the plus side they give us three squares a day and the guns were fun. So was the hand-to-hand combat training. I learned some good tricks."

"Yeah? Maybe a sparring match is in order."

"Maybe give me another year to practice. What about you, anyone try to kill you lately?"

"Not for a week or so."

Jonny's laugh slowly died when no one else joined in. "Shit, you're serious. What was it this time, more religious nuts?"

"I wish. It was a giant three-headed elemental monster called a chimera. The monster tried to burn me, drown me, and crush me. I came through it okay, but it was a near thing for Kelsie."

Jonny turned his gaze on Kelsie. "He's a dangerous guy to hang around with. Did he tell you about the time we were almost eaten by these big black dogs?"

Prime chose that moment to come flying out of his bedroom. "Master, your friend's lack of knowledge regarding the shadow hounds is appalling. I felt it was my duty to come and explain."

To Jonny's credit his reaction to seeing a talking book with the face of a demon was limited to his eyes nearly bugging out of his head. "What the fuck is that?"

"I thought I mentioned Prime in my last letter. He's my scholomantic slash familiar. Long story. Let's just say my year was a good deal less boring than I might have liked. On the plus side I picked up several great friends." For the sake of not totally overwhelming his already overwhelmed friend Conryu didn't mention Cerberus or the Dark Lady.

Kelsie blushed and Prime cleared his nonexistent throat. "Thank you, Master."

"Don't mention it, or the shadow hounds for that matter, but if you want to hang out in the living room it's fine."

Prime settled on the coffee table just as Maria pushed the door open. Her arms were laden with bags and a pizza box. Conryu and Jonny both jumped up to help her with her burden. To no one's surprise Jonny made off with the pizza box.

Jonny took a deep breath and sighed. "This is what I missed the most."

"Hey!" Conryu punched him in the arm.

"Sorry, second most."

Kelsie came to join them in the kitchen as they emptied bags of food on the counter. She whispered, "You are so lucky. I never had friends like this. Jonny seems nice."

"Yeah, he's awesome."

Everyone gathered their snacks of choice. Pizza and chips for Conryu and Jonny while Kelsie and Maria swapped the chips for a salad. Everyone settled around the tv. He sat between the girls on the couch and Jonny returned to the recliner.

Conryu switched the baseball game on. The Sentinel Soldiers were down three runs to the Stark Sturgeons.

"Good to see some things never change," Jonny said around a mouthful of pizza. "The bums still don't know how to play ball."

The Soldiers hadn't made it to the Alliance Series since before Conryu was born and they hadn't even made it to the playoffs in ten years. The screen went black for a second before a giant, flashing alert sign appeared followed by a sternly attractive female anchorwoman.

"We interrupt this broadcast with an important announcement. This station has received a recording from the terrorist organization known as the Le Fay Society. We made this available to the city government one hour ago and after they viewed it we were assured everything is under control. Please keep that in mind as we play the message. Some of you may find it disturbing. If there are small children in the room now would be a good time to take them out."

Thirty seconds later the screen flickered and the image of a woman in an Imperial-style dragon mask appeared on the screen. "I am Lady Dragon, interim leader of the Le Fay Society. My agents have planted a number of magical weapons in Sentinel City. If our true leader, Morgana Le Fay, is not released from the Lonely Rock Prison and the abomination Conryu Koda handed over to us within forty-eight hours we will unleash an army of shadow beasts that will slaughter your people by the thousands. There will be no negotiations. You will comply or die. We will contact you every twelve hours until our demands are met."

The anchor reappeared. "The mayor has assured us that the Department of Magic has this matter well under control and the people of the city are in no danger."

When she started talking about him, Conryu turned the tv off.

"Is this what Dad had you working on?" Maria asked.

Conryu found his appetite gone despite the steaming slice of pizza in front of him. "That seems like a safe bet, though he never told me anything specific about a threat."

"He wouldn't have. Dad wouldn't want you any more deeply involved in something like this than was absolutely necessary."

Outside, sirens came screaming closer and his phone rang. He answered while Kelsie ran to the window.

"There're six cop cars out here and men with machine guns are spilling out," she said.

"Hello." Conryu only half listened to what Kelsie was saying. "Angus? Calm down. What do you mean I need to get out of the building?"

* * *

Orin watched the recording for the fifth time. He was sitting in the Department conference room, waiting for the mayor and his crisis team to arrive. City hall had sent the Society's ultimatum over ten minutes ago demanding to know if it was a hoax and if it wasn't what he was doing about it.

He'd put them off by claiming he didn't want to talk about it over the phone. That bought him however long it would take the officials to make the trip from City Hall three blocks north of here. He turned the computer off and leaned back in his chair. They'd all known something like this was coming, despite his assurances to the contrary. He hadn't exactly lied to the mayor, but he had indicated they were making more progress than they actually were.

Beside him, Terra, Lin, and Angus sat in stunned silence. Finally Terra said, "The other world governments will never agree to free Morgana. She's the most dangerous terrorist on the planet. Nothing we, the mayor, or the president for that matter, can say will change anything."

Orin rubbed his face. "I don't disagree. What I need now is something I can tell the mayor that will give him confidence that we can handle this without giving in to their demands."

He looked desperately at each of them, but found nothing to give him hope. Lin looked exhausted, his eyes black and bloodshot with three days of stubble on his chin. Terra was only a little better, her complexion paler than usual and her gray-blond hair in disarray. Angus just looked totally confused.

Terra shook her head. "I have nothing to offer you, Orin. We've done everything possible and it came up short. What we need to do now is plan for the upcoming battle, try to figure out how to save as many lives as possible."

"That's not what he's going to want to hear."

Orin's secretary spoke through the loud speaker. "The mayor and his team have arrived, sir."

"Speak of the devil." Orin heaved himself out of his chair.

The others joined him and a moment later the doors swung open. The mayor strode through looking for all the world like he owned the place. Tom Corbin was a hale and fit fifty-year-old who favored gray suits and expensive shoes. The Corbin family had been the heart of Sentinel City politics for the past hundred years and if Tom had his way it would continue to be for another hundred.

Behind him were the commandant of police, fire marshal, a pair of security guards, and two others, a man and a woman, that Orin had never met.

"Tom." Orin held out his hand, curious to find out if his old friend would take it.

"Orin." They shook and Orin had a moment of relief. "Please tell me these lunatics are bluffing."

"I'm sorry, Tom. Despite our best efforts we've been unable to neutralize the threat."

Tom sat in the nearest chair and waved his people down. When everyone had settled in he said, "That's not remotely acceptable. I've spoken to the president and there's no way they'll free the witch Morgana. Even worse, the war up north is still raging. We can expect no help from Central."

"That was our thinking as well, sir. I've contacted all the combat-worthy wizards, not that there are many, in the city, including my wife. They're ready to fight at the first sign of danger. We also have an estimate of the most-threatened areas. Evacuations may be prudent."

The unfamiliar woman put her hands on the table and leaned forward. "Our view is that evacuations will be ineffective if shadow beasts are involved. Once summoned they will be free to hunt anywhere in the city once the sun sets."

"Who, exactly, are you?" Orin asked.

"Maggie Chin. My colleague and I are magical risk consultants. Analyzing the potential threat of a large-scale event is our specialty."

"Are you a wizard?" Terra asked.

Orin had been wondering the same thing since she didn't have a gray robe, though Shizuku often wore suits when she was working.

"No, I'm an analyst, not a wizard. But that in no way invalidates my conclusion. The risk of panic outweighs any gain from an evacuation."

Orin drew a breath to continue the argument but Tom raised his hand. "We're of one mind on this matter so let's leave it there."

Orin clenched his jaw and nodded. "Of course. What about organizing a defense?"

Tom glanced at his consultant who looked at the tablet on the desk in front of her. "Conventional weapons are useless against magical threats and our inventory of enchanted weapons is exceedingly limited as is our force of wizards. We will do what we can, but unless the terrorists can be convinced to stay their hand, our options are limited."

Orin looked from the consultant to Tom. "I'm not certain I understand what you're planning."

"Tell me about Conryu Koda," Tom said.

Acid burned the back of Orin's throat. "Conryu's a good kid. He's been of great help in our efforts to resolve this matter."

"And you think he'll continue to be willing to help?"

"Absolutely. Why?"

"We're planning to take him into protective custody. If we can't come up with an alternative solution we'll offer him to the Society in hopes of convincing them to give us more time to meet their other demand."

"You're going to sacrifice him?" Orin kept his emotions under control by the narrowest of margins.

"The life of one or the lives of thousands. It's not a difficult decision." Maggie's emotionless tone grated on his nerves.

"And if you turn over our best hope of defeating this enemy and they activate the spell anyway, what then?"

Tom shook his head. "Even if it's one in a million, it's a chance we have to take."

Angus leapt to his feet. "This is madness. That boy's value is beyond measure."

The mayor didn't even spare Angus a glance. "The decision's been made. We've already sent officers to take him into custody. I know you're fond of the boy, Orin, but I have to do what I think is best for the city."

Angus's face had turned red and he was working himself into a fury. Orin wasn't far behind, but he'd learned better control. He also had an idea. Before Angus blew his top Orin grabbed the professor by the collar and dragged him toward the door.

"If you can't control yourself you can wait in your office." Orin leaned in close and whispered, "Warn him, Angus."

He tossed the professor out into the hall and pulled the door shut. "Sorry about that. Angus has always been a little temperamental. Shall we discuss contingency plans?"

* * *

"They're coming for you, my boy. The mayor means to use you as a bribe to convince the terrorists to spare the city, though Orin assures me there's no hope of that happening. You need to hurry. The police are already on their way."

"Actually they're here. Thanks for the warning, Angus." Conryu disconnected.

"What's going on?" Maria asked.

"It appears I'm to be a sacrificial lamb. We need to split, now."

"No way we're sneaking out." Jonny had joined Kelsie at the window. "Those guys are the city's elite counter-terrorism unit. They're the best."

"Shit! Well, there are other options. I can go by dark portal."

"Mom's wards won't let you open one in the building."

"Reveal!" A shimmering wall of light magic appeared beyond the window. "Is your mom home from her job?"

Maria nodded. "She got in late last night. I don't think she's up yet and even if she was it would take hours to open a gap in the barrier."

"Not for me it won't. Would you apologize for me?" Conryu motioned Kelsie and Jonny away from the window and held up both hands. He wasn't supposed to do a breaking without a circle, but under the circumstances he didn't have any choice.

Maria grabbed his arm. "What are you going to do?"

"I'm going to blow a hole in the wards and split."

"Not without me," Jonny said.

"Or me," Kelsie added.

"This is nuts," Maria said. "But I'm with you too."

"No. I doubt you'd survive a trip through Hell. Go to your mom and tell her what's happening then head to the Department. I'll be in touch as soon as I can." Conryu tossed his cellphone on the couch where it sank down between the cushions. It'd be too easy for the police to track him with it. "Prime!"

"Coming, Master."

Maria grabbed the front of his shirt, yanked his head down, and kissed him hard on the lips. When they finally came up for air she said, "Don't you dare get yourself killed."

"I sense people coming, Master. Six, no ten."

"A breaching team," Jonny added.

"Right, time to go." Conryu raised his hands again. "Break!"

The barrier shattered.

"Your friend will need protection, Master. He has no alignment to dark magic."

Conryu grabbed Jonny's arm. "Cloak of Darkness!"

When the liquid darkness had covered Jonny from head to toe Conryu turned to Prime. "Portal spell."

"Yes, Master."

The words of the spell appeared in his mind and he chanted. "Reveal the way through infinite darkness. Open the path, Hell Portal!"

The swirling black disk appeared in front of him. Conryu grabbed Jonny and Kelsie, pulled them through, and willed the gate to close behind them.

* * *

Maria's nausea faded along with the dark portal. He was gone and once more she couldn't follow. How many times was she going to have to watch Conryu run into danger without her? Though she understood there was no way she'd survive a trip through Hell with him. One step through that portal and she would have dropped dead.

There was a knock on the door. "Police! Open up!"

She sighed, crossed the room, and opened the door. The shiny black barrels of two guns were pointed straight at her head. She yelped and took a step back.

The officers pushed the door open and rushed into the apartment. Two men in bulletproof vests, dark-blue fatigues, and helmets held her at gunpoint while the rest searched from room to room.

The Kodas' apartment wasn't huge and a minute later someone shouted, "Clear!"

The living room was filled to bursting with ten large men and Maria. One of the officers removed his helmet and approached her.

"Where is he?"

"Conryu left."

"Bullshit! There's no way he snuck past us. Where's he hiding?"

"Maria! What's going on?"

She slumped with relief at the sight of her mother approaching from down the hall. It looked like she'd just thrown on a robe and slippers. She must have sensed when Conryu broke her wards.

The officer that had been interrogating her spun and leveled his weapon at her mom. A flick of her wrist sent the machine gun flying along with both of the weapons pointed at Maria.

The officer started to reach for the pistol at his side. Mom just glared at him as if daring him to try it.

He seemed to decide discretion was the better part of valor. "You need to keep your distance, ma'am. This is an active scene."

"I don't appreciate people pointing guns at my daughter, Officer." Mom waved her over and Maria ran out of the apartment and hugged her. "Now what's this all about?"

"I have orders to take Conryu Koda into custody. I believe your daughter has relevant information."

Mom looked down at her. "Do you know where he is?"

"No. I tried to tell them. Conryu left."

"As I said, there's no way he slipped past my men." The officer crossed his arms. "Now tell me the truth."

"How did he leave, Maria?"

"By dark portal."

"That's what I thought." Mom turned her gaze on the officer. "Did your superiors fail to mention Conryu is a wizard? Traveling by dark portal he could be anywhere in the city in half a second."

"I was told he's only a first-year wizard and advanced spells were beyond his current ability."

Mom laughed. "Conryu is the most powerful wizard in history. No spell is beyond his ability. Whoever gave you your briefing was woefully ignorant of who you're dealing with."

"Sir," one of the other officers said. "Ops reports they've tracked his cell phone to the apartment."

"You still claim he's not here?"

Maria let go of her mother and turned around. "On the couch."

A third officer bent down and pulled it out of the cushions. "Cellphone, sir. Locked."

The muscle in the officer's jaw bunched. "Fuck! Wrap it up, boys. As usual, the brass gave us bad intel. I'm going to have to ask you to come with us."

He reached out to grab Maria. Mom moved in front of her. "Do you have a warrant to arrest my daughter?"

"No, ma'am, but she's a material witness. We may have more questions."

"If you do we'll be at the Department of Magic with my husband. Feel free to contact us there."

He let out a little growl but finally nodded. "Alright."

The commander and his men retrieved their weapons and filed past Maria and her mother down the hall. Mom kept her arms around Maria until they were all out of sight. "Tell me everything."

Maria did as her mother asked and when she finished she added, "He wanted me to tell you he was sorry about smashing your wards."

Her mother waved her hand. "He didn't destroy them, just opened a hole in them. I can fix them in an afternoon. We need to see your father. Clearly more is afoot here than we know."

* * *

Conryu, Prime, Kelsie, and Jonny hung in the black nothingness of the area between the mortal realm and Hell. Kelsie grabbed on to him and trembled while Jonny spun in a slow circle, taking it all in.

Cerberus barked as he ran up to them. Kelsie squeaked and tried to hide behind him. The giant three-headed dog towered over the little group.

"Dude, please tell me that's a friend of yours." Jonny and Cerberus eyed each other.

"Cerberus is my guardian demon. Aren't you, boy?"

The demon dog barked again and lowered one of his heads

so Conryu could give him a scratch. Conryu looked down at Kelsie. "You can pet him. Cerberus won't bite unless I tell him to."

Kelsie reached out a hesitant hand and stroked Cerberus's massive chest. Cerberus panted as she rubbed him. When Jonny moved closer the demon dog let out a deep growl, stopping his friend cold.

"He has no connection to dark magic," Prime said in answer to Conryu's unspoken question. "Demons and ordinary humans don't always see eye to eye. You shouldn't dawdle here, Master. Even protected, spending too much time in Hell isn't a good idea for non-dark-aligned individuals."

"I second that," Jonny said.

Conryu looked up at Cerberus. "Can you guide us to my father's dojo?"

Cerberus barked and trotted off. They flew along behind him for half a minute before he stopped.

"This is a bad idea," Jonny said. "Those cops will look there for you next."

"I have to let Dad know what's happening. Five minutes tops. He should be between classes so no one will see us."

Conryu cast the portal spell again and they stepped out onto the sparring floor. Dad was kneeling in front of the room facing the ancient swords in his black training uniform. He stood and turned to face them, a deep frown creasing his usually calm face.

"What has happened?"

"Long story, Dad." Conryu gave him the condensed version. "So basically I'm being hunted by the police so they can turn me over to the people who've been trying to kill me for the last year. I figure the only way out of this mess is to deal with the terrorists myself."

"Can you?"

Trust his father to come straight to the point. "Not sure. Mr. Kane was a little vague with what was happening when I helped him this winter. I believe the boxes we were looking for are the weapons they mentioned on the news. If I can neutralize them then I should be safe, along with the city. Whatever I do, I have only two days to get it done."

"How can I help?"

"I need to talk to Terra and Mr. Kane. Can you carry a message to them?"

"Of course. I need to speak to your mother as well. If she finds out about this some other way she'll be even more upset. I'll take your message to the Department."

"Actually, Mr. Koda, if you pick up a cheap prepaid cellphone and sneak it in to them we could keep in touch without the police knowing."

Everyone looked at Jonny. "What? We studied urban escape and survival in school."

"How will I get you the number?" Dad asked.

"We need one as well. Why don't we go together? That way we can just exchange numbers." Jonny pulled out his wallet and opened it. Moths didn't fly out, but it was empty just the same. "I'm broke."

Conryu had thirty bucks. They looked at Kelsie who shrugged. "I left my purse at your apartment."

"I have enough for both," Dad said. "Let me change and we'll go. Put the closed sign up."

Jonny jogged over to the door while his father went to the locker room. When he'd flipped the sign Jonny said, "We shouldn't all go together. I'll go with your dad and meet you guys at Giovanni's."

Conryu shook his head. "We had their food boxes all over the apartment. If the cops are on the ball they'll be keeping an eye out for us there. What about the Burger Shack on Third?"

"That'll work."

Conryu and Kelsie left by the back door. He had until Jonny rejoined them to figure out how to do in two days what the Department of Magic had failed to do in a year.

Chapter 3

Spy Stuff

Maria and her mom drove to the Department and went upstairs to her father's office. They'd only taken long enough for her mother to dress and collect her satchel before they left. She didn't even take time to restore the wards. Mom insisted they were sufficient for the moment and she was eager to talk to Dad.

Maria had been to the Department building several times over the years and it was always a bustling place. Today everyone was subdued, their heads hanging, and unwilling to make eye contact.

Outside the office Dad's secretary was gone. There was no sign of the woman's purse and her computer was turned off. Maria glanced over at her mother. "Something's really wrong."

"Yes. I've never seen Daphne away from her desk. She's devoted to your father." Mom strode forward and shoved the door open.

Inside, Dad, Terra, and a man she didn't know sat around her father's big desk staring out the window. Of all the things she'd expected Dad and Terra to be doing, "nothing" was at the bottom of the list. Dad came around his desk and hugged them.

"What are you two doing here?"

"A better question," Mom said, "is what were a bunch of cops with machine guns doing at our building? What's this stupidity about handing Conryu over to the Society? And why aren't you doing something about it?"

Dad looked so exhausted at that moment Maria hugged him again.

"Thank you, sweetheart. We've been removed and confined to my office following Conryu's escape. The mayor and his people are handling matters now. They seem to think we're too sympathetic to their prey."

"Is Tom really foolish enough to think handing Conryu over will accomplish anything? I saw a replay of the recording. He's just a bonus. Morgana's who they really want."

"I know and I explained it to Tom in just those terms, but the president made it clear there was no way they'd free Morgana. At this point he's desperate enough to believe whatever those two advisors tell him. He sees Conryu as his only hope of saving his city. When he escaped, well, Tom didn't take it very well."

"So what are we going to do to help Conryu?" Maria stood with her hands on her hips. She knew her father was in a difficult position, but she'd rather die than sit there and do nothing.

"I'm not certain there's anything we can do." Dad went back around his desk and dropped into his chair.

"That's nonsense." Maria needed to get everyone off their asses and working again. "We're a formidable group. You've been investigating this business for a while, right? No one tells me much, but I've picked up enough details to know this isn't something that just came up."

"The problem is," Terra said. "We've exhausted all the avenues of inquiry and come up empty. The boxes remain hidden and until they're neutralized Conryu remains in danger."

"Great, so he has two days to save himself and the city with no one but Jonny and Kelsie to help. All we can do, the people who care about him most, is sit on our hands and hope." Maria wanted to cry.

"Two days, you said." Terra pursed her lips. "That's not right. Lin, we need your laptop."

"It's in my office. The mayor said we aren't supposed to leave this room."

"There aren't any guards," Maria said.

"It's not that far away," Terra added. "I can't see why they'd care. If you're too scared I'll go."

She started to stand, but Lin waved her back. "I'll go. If one of us is going to be locked up, better me than you."

Terra snorted. "As if they could hold a wizard that didn't wish to be held."

Lin left the office and Dad asked, "What are you thinking?"

"Based on the speed of the island it will enter and exit the potential zone of activation over the course of a day. If I'm right Mercia could possibly activate the boxes within twenty-four hours rather than forty-eight."

Mara stared. "You mean Conryu only has one day?"

"Less than that actually. I can't give you any accurate numbers until I run my theory through Lin's program."

* * *

Conryu conjured a tiny Cloak of Darkness spell and shaped it to look like sunglasses. As disguises went it was pretty pathetic, but just walking around without so much as a hat made him feel exposed. Prime had shifted so he resembled a simple, if ugly, book and Conryu carried him tucked under one arm.

The streets were quiet as they made their way toward Third and the Burger Shack where they were supposed to meet Jonny. Conryu hoped they didn't run into any trouble. Not that Dad and Jonny couldn't take care of themselves, but against guns they'd be in a tight space.

They stopped at a crosswalk and waited for the light to change. "You have a plan, right?" Kelsie asked. She sounded so optimistic he hated to burst her bubble.

"I have an idea, whether it's nonsense or workable we'll have to wait and see. Either way I don't intend to give myself up."

"I don't think you should. I can't imagine the government being willing to turn an innocent citizen over to terrorists on the off chance they might do the right thing. It seems as criminal as what the Society is pulling."

The light changed and they crossed over along with the small group that had gathered. Five minutes later the restaurant came into view. Across from it was a green bench beside a trash bin. The bench offered a good view in both directions and no one was close enough to eavesdrop on them.

"Let's sit here."

They settled in to wait for Jonny. Conryu held Prime on his lap, angled away from the street so no one would notice him speaking. Kelsie sat close to him like she was his girlfriend, letting him keep his voice down while they talked.

"Okay, Prime, we need to find those boxes. This winter we theorized they were moved through dark portals. Is there any way we can track where they went?"

"No, Master."

"Damn it." That had been his one good idea.

"Not in the human realm at least. If we go to the starting location Cerberus may be able to track where they went through Hell. We can then emerge and recover the items in this world."

"Are you sure that will work?" Kelsie asked.

"Not at all. I'm not aware of something like this ever being done before."

"It gives us a starting point at least. Next problem. Will the spells I know be enough to deal with any shadow beasts we encounter?"

"No, Master. Dark magic works mainly through entropy. Shadow beasts are already dead and have no physical form to decay. Domination will allow you to control them, but I have no spells that will destroy them. Fire and light magic would be best."

"I can work with that. Last thing. If we run into those cops again I need a nonlethal way to disable them quickly."

Prime opened and flipped through his pages, eventually landing on a spell called Reaper's Gale. Just the name gave Conryu a chill. He started to read and Kelsie moved in closer to follow along.

The spell drained the life force of anyone caught in the effect. He read the words over and over, committing them to memory.

"This looks lethal," Conryu said when he finished memorizing the spell.

"If you cast it at your full power it absolutely is." Prime snapped shut. "But if you modulate it, whisper, use a flick of your wrist instead of a full swing, and most importantly, focus your will on not killing anyone, it will serve your needs admirably."

Kelsie glanced at him. "Do you have any idea how terrifying it is to know just how easy it would be for you to wipe out scores of people with a wave of your hand?"

"Yeah. I think about it before every spell I cast."

Jonny ambled down the street ten minutes later and waved to them. When he reached the bench Conryu and Kelsie got to their feet and they started down the sidewalk. One of the locations he'd helped clear this winter was only half a mile away. It wouldn't take them long to figure out if his theory was workable or not.

"Did you have any trouble at the electronics shop?" Kelsie asked.

"Not a bit, though your dad's wallet is lighter by a hundred and twenty bucks."

"I didn't think prepaid phones were that expensive."

"They're not." Jonny dug the cheap little flip phone out of his pocket and showed it to Conryu. "He offered me an extra forty to help tide us over."

That gave them seventy with what he had in his wallet. Since Conryu didn't expect to have to do much shopping it should be plenty. One way or the other this business would be settled in two days.

* * *

As the little group walked along toward the abandoned building Conryu found his gaze darting left and right, checking every person they passed for a reaction. Either no one watched the news or they all had other things on their mind. It helped that the majority of the people around them kept their heads down and were absorbed in whatever was on their phones.

As much as his father hated it when everyone was distracted, right now it struck Conryu as the best trend ever. If they'd had to travel everywhere by dark portal it would have been hard on Jonny. Should it come to that, Conryu planned to ask his friend to sit the rest of the mission out.

The condemned building looked exactly as he remembered only without snow. Yellow police tape blocked the entrance, but Jonny just ripped it off and shoved his way inside. The little niche that had held the box was now plainly visible and a fresh selection of beer bottles littered the floor. The sour stench of alcohol and piss perfumed the interior. Without the ward the punks that partied here must have returned.

Kelsie put her hand over her face. "Oh my god, it stinks in here. Who would come to such a place for fun?"

"The smell's a lot easier to tolerate if you're drunk or high." Jonny looked at the dump and crinkled his nose. "Pity I'm completely sober right now."

"Can you stand it for a little longer?" Conryu asked. "It would probably be safest if I try and locate the box on my own. If I find it I'll come back for you two."

"Not planning on ditching me again are you, bro?"

"I want to go too," Kelsie said.

"I appreciate that, guys, really, but if it takes me a while to find the new location I don't want you to have to spend any more time in Hell than necessary. Especially you, Jonny. I have no idea what excessive exposure to dark energy would do to a non-wizard."

"Accelerated aging and cellular breakdown." Prime flew up out of his grasp and hovered in the middle of the room. "Long-term exposure will literally rot a normal human from the inside out."

Kelsie grimaced. "Yuck."

Jonny crossed his arms and for a moment Conryu feared he might want to argue. "Fine, but you better come back and get me before you do anything stupid."

Conryu held out a fist and Jonny bumped it.

"Promise," Conryu said. "If there's stupid stuff to be done, we'll do it together."

He turned and held his hand out. "Reveal the way through infinite darkness. Open the path, Hell Portal!"

The black disk appeared and Conryu stepped through it with Prime beside him. When the portal had closed Prime turned to face him. "Those two are a liability, Master, especially the boy."

Conryu sighed and reached out to stroke Cerberus's side. He didn't know exactly how the giant dog appeared beside him without Conryu noticing, but he'd become so used to it he didn't even jump.

"I know, you're right, but they're my friends and they're trying to help. If I tell them they're just in the way I'll damage two very important relationships."

"If you don't, you might get them killed."

"Yeah." No arguing with that. "Let's focus on the matter at hand. If we can't locate the boxes this problem is moot. Cerberus."

The demon dog focused all six eyes on him.

"I need you to track something for me. A magical artifact was moved from here through a dark portal. Can you follow it?"

Cerberus raised his heads and waved them around, mouths open and noses sniffing. He padded around, a little this way, a little that way, until he finally barked and crouched down.

It didn't take a genius to interpret that. Conryu leapt onto Cerberus's back, snatched Prime out of the air, and they were off. Cerberus bounded through the darkness, sniffing as he ran.

It seemed they hadn't gone any distance when Cerberus stopped and barked again.

"Here, huh?" Conryu looked around, but it wasn't like there were any landmarks to help him figure out where he was. He didn't know how demons did it. "Guess we'll just have to take a peek."

Conryu raised his hand to cast the portal spell again, but Prime stopped him. "If there are protections in place it would be wise to look before we leap."

He climbed down off Cerberus. "Okay. How do we do that?"

Prime opened and his pages flipped. When he stopped, Conryu read the spell. Vision Gate. That sounded useful. "Grant me the power to see through realms, Vision Gate!"

The darkness swirled, though the effect was more psychic than visual. Three seconds later a round portal appeared and through it he saw a pedestal with one of the boxes sitting on it. He reached up and patted Cerberus. "Good boy. Reveal!"

Lines of dark energy appeared in his enhanced sight. Plenty of wards, though considerably less than he'd expected. He willed the view to pull back. The new location had stone walls and was almost as dark as Hell. The view shifted again, this time top down. Beside the pedestal was a channel with brackish water running through it.

"Great. Of course it's in the sewer." Something moved further down the tunnel and a moment later a pair of great black hounds padded into view. "They look familiar."

Cerberus growled deep in his chest.

"Shadow hounds, Master. It's good that we scouted the area first."

"It certainly is."

A couple minutes passed as he sent the viewing portal all around the area near the box. There was no sign of any more guardians. Two shadow beasts wouldn't be a problem for him now.

"Let's do this." Conryu raised his hand.

"What about your promise to retrieve your friends before going after the box?" Prime asked.

"I will, but first I'm going to kill those shadow hounds."

He opened the portal twenty yards from the hounds and stepped through. They must have sensed his presence. Conryu had barely cleared the portal when two pairs of red eyes raced towards him.

"All things burn to ash, Inferno Blast!" Searing white flames blasted from his hand, filling the tunnel and obliterating the hounds. He allowed a full minute before he stepped back into the portal.

"That was impressive, Master. I've seen fire wizards that couldn't conjure flames that intense."

"Thanks."

Cerberus took them back to where they started and Conryu opened another portal.

"Did you find it?" Kelsie asked the instant he emerged in the condemned building.

He nodded, feeling a little queasy. Casting that many spells in such close succession was enough to exhaust even him. He needed to rest, but first the box. He'd be damned before he let whoever was behind this move it again.

"There are some wards protecting it so you two need to stay behind me until we deal with them. Hold still, Jonny."

His friend stopped pacing long enough for Conryu to cast Cloak of Darkness.

"I should warn you the box is in the sewer. If you think it stinks here just wait a second."

Moments later they were standing a safe distance from the pedestal. Kelsie summoned a flame sphere to light the place up. Jonny shook his head. "All this fuss over that thing?"

Conryu had to admit the black box wasn't terribly impressive on its own, but he knew the power of the artifact inside. He crossed his fingers and wrists. "Darkness dispels everything."

He hurled the black sphere, which exploded on impact, wiping all the protections away. He waited ten seconds more just to be sure.

"I think we're good," Kelsie said.

Conryu agreed and they strode over to collect their prize. His spell had blasted off the necroplasma, revealing the clean wood beneath. He flipped the lid open and inside was a black gem half the size of his fist. Instead of sparkling in the firelight the gem seemed to absorb it.

"It must be worth a fortune." Jonny reached out to touch the gem.

"Stop!" Conryu, Kelsie, and Prime all shouted at the same time.

Jonny jerked his hand back. "What?"

"Never touch a magical artifact until you're sure what will happen," Conryu said.

"It's one of the first things they teach us," Kelsie added.

Conryu put his hand over the gem. "Shatter!"

It burst into tiny black flakes. All the magic stored in the gem vanished.

He snapped the lid shut. "I bet Terra would like to have a look at this. What do you say we get out of here?"

* * *

When Lady Raven felt something drawing near one of her artifacts she assumed it was another sewer worker and her shadow hounds would deal with the intruder shortly. Sure enough seconds after she became aware of the presence it vanished. That was the third unfortunate to stumble on her hiding place. Not too bad considering it had been there for six months.

She stretched out on her couch and returned her attention to the tv. It had been an amusing few hours, listening to the city's leaders lie and make excuses as they tried to reassure the people that there was really nothing to worry about. That the Society wouldn't do something so horrible. Even the idiot men running the city couldn't be stupid enough to believe the threat was a bluff. All the mayor needed to do was ask the Department of Magic and he'd learn the truth.

No, it was all propaganda to keep the people calm. If the leaders of the world failed to do as they were told, they'd learn what the Society was capable of. While Lady Raven dearly wanted to help release their imprisoned leader, a part of her wanted the deadline to pass, freeing her to activate her artifacts and watch hundreds of shadow beasts overrun the city.

She sensed another presence and less than a minute later gasped as a sharp pain stabbed her chest. One of the artifacts had been destroyed.

Even if the incompetents from the Department somehow located her new hiding places they didn't have power enough between them to overcome the protections she'd woven around them.

Her stomach twisted. It had to be him.

Lady Raven leapt off the couch and marched to her casting chamber. Ignoring everything else she went straight to her scrying mirror. She focused her will, but when the cloudy depths of the mirror cleared, only an empty pedestal appeared.

With a massive effort she restrained herself from smashing the mirror to shards. If the boxes were in danger she needed to increase her defenses. She paced from one end of the chamber to the other. What could she do that would slow the abomination down?

Two shadow hounds were obviously not enough. It would be a simple matter to summon more, but she doubted that would do it. It was time to call in a few markers. Lady Raven had made more than her share of allies in Hell, done them favors, and it was time to cash in her IOUs.

That left one more matter. Did she dare tell the Hierarchs that the project was in danger now that they were within hours of success?

Not yet. If the boy forced his way past her enhanced defenses once more then she'd alert her superiors. Better to seek help than allow the enterprise to fail completely. It might cost her a promotion, but that was a small price compared to a swift execution.

* * *

Maria paced while Lin and Terra fiddled with the computer. Despite the warnings no one had bothered Lin on his trip to and from his office. In fact, he said he hadn't seen another soul. It appeared those in charge had ordered the building cleared. For some reason Maria found that disconcerting. A couple hundred people worked for the Department. Even—make that especially—if there was a crisis you'd think there would be plenty for everyone to do.

It felt like they were trying to hide what was happening.

"Would you please sit down?" Dad said. "You're making me even more nervous."

"Sorry, but if I sit I'll fidget. I just realized I haven't seen Angus. He's the one that called Conryu. I figured they'd have him locked up with the rest of us."

"I haven't seen him since this morning." Dad sighed and shook his head. "Angus is surprisingly sneaky and has a tendency to show up or disappear when you least expect it. My guess is he's holed up somewhere, staying out of sight. Hopefully, just this once, he'll keep out of trouble."

Terra slammed her fist on the desk. "I knew it! Based on my calculations Mercia will be able to activate the boxes in sixteen hours and the island should move out of range in another forty."

Maria stopped in her tracks. "Conryu thinks he has two days."

Terra nodded. "If he finds one of the boxes and neutralizes it Mercia will know and she'll activate the other four as soon as she's able."

Lin started typing and Terra looked down at him. "What are you doing?"

"Research. I'm curious about the mayor's advisors. Something about those two struck me as off."

"I didn't sense anything magical."

"It's a cop thing, instincts maybe, I don't know, but I've learned to trust the feeling. Besides, it's not like we have anything else to do."

Twenty minutes later the office doors opened. Every gaze turned to watch Conryu's father walk through. He carried himself with this sort of Zen calm, even in the face of calamity.

"Is he okay?" Maria asked the moment the doors closed.

Sho turned his gaze on her father and raised an eyebrow.

"It's okay, we checked for bugs and magical eavesdropping. You can talk freely here."

"My son is fine and determined to do what he can to set this business right." Sho dug around in his pants pocket, finally emerging with a small flip phone. "This is prepaid and has the number of a matching phone programmed into it. I don't know what he intends. This magical business is beyond me."

"How's Connie taking it?" her mother asked.

"As well as can be expected when her son is being hunted by the police so he can be made into a sacrifice." Sho's voice was as hard as Maria had ever heard it. "How has this fallen on Conryu's shoulders? Surely there are others better equipped to handle such a crisis."

"Mr. Koda, my name is Terra Pane. I'm a wizard working at the Department. I tested your son when he was first discovered to have wizard potential and later I saw him using that power. Despite his youth and inexperience I believe Conryu has a better chance to resolve this matter than anyone. Frankly, if he fails, this city will be turned into a charnel house."

Sho gave a slight shake of his head. "It's too much to ask of him. He's still just a boy."

Maria closed the distance between them. "You're wrong. I've seen firsthand who Conryu's become over the past year. He can do this. I believe in him and you should too."

The phone rang cutting Sho off. He handed it to Maria who flipped it open. "Conryu? Okay, I'll put it on speaker."

She hit the button and set the phone on her father's desk. "Go ahead."

"I found the first box. It was hidden about a mile from its original location. The wards were minimal, but there were two shadow beasts guarding it. Nothing too powerful."

"How did you find it?" Terra asked.

"Cerberus tracked the residual energy of the transference spell. Don't ask me how exactly."

"You summoned the demon dog to our realm?" Terra's voice rose and her eyes grew wide.

"No, sorry, I should have been more specific. We tracked it through Hell. Prime says enchanted energy lingers longer in the magical realms. Anyway, I'm feeling pretty good about our chances of finding the rest of the boxes."

"Conryu, this is very important," Terra said. "Don't disturb or dispel the boxes until you've located all five."

"Uh, wish I'd known that five minutes ago. I already broke the wards and smashed the artifact inside. Is that bad?"

Nervous looks were passed around the office. Finally Terra said, "It's not bad, but it does start the clock ticking. Mercia will know you've destroyed the box. I fear she will now activate the summoning as soon as the island is within range."

"I've got like forty hours left, no sweat."

"No, you have sixteen hours."

"Shit! Are you sure?"

"It might be less, but certainly not more," Terra said. "You have to hurry."

"No kidding. You want me to send you the box and what's left of the artifact?"

"Please. Leave it outside somewhere and we'll retrieve it."

"I can leave it under Mom's car beside the back wheel."

"That's fine. Hurry, Conryu. We're counting on you."

"And be careful," Maria added before the line went dead.

Chapter 4

Recovery

Conryu disconnected the phone and fought a sudden wave of exhaustion. They'd left the sewer by the nearest manhole, rather than by portal, and made their way to a park across the street. He'd feared on the walk over he might not make it. His relief upon seeing a bench was pathetic.

The first hint of a backlash headache was forming behind his eyes. Kelsie and Jonny were both looking at him with nervous gazes. If he looked as bad as he felt he doubted he projected confidence.

"That didn't sound good," Kelsie said. "Sixteen hours isn't very long to track down four more boxes."

"No. I need to minimize my magic use so I'll have strength enough when I really need it. Jonny, could you do me a favor and run the box over to the Department? You know Mom's car. She parks in the Science Department's lot. You shouldn't have any trouble finding it." Conryu handed him the phone and box.

"No problem. What about you two?"

"I need to rest. By the time you get back I should be good to go after the second box."

"Cool, later." Jonny gave him one last look and jogged off toward the street.

Kelsie patted her lap. "Lie down and close your eyes. I'll keep watch."

Conryu took her up on the suggestion, letting his legs dangle off the end of the bench and holding Prime on his chest. He sighed and closed his eyes, thoroughly glad Maria couldn't see him right then.

"Can we do this?" Kelsie asked.

Conryu opened one eye and looked up at her. "Do we have another choice?"

"We could hide. She said we had less than a day. It wouldn't be hard to avoid the police for that long. When the time was up they'd be too busy to bother with us."

"Too busy trying to keep regular people from getting killed by hundreds of shadow beasts. Which I know from experience is impossible for someone without magic. It's the responsibility of those with the power to make a difference to do so."

"You don't even want to be a wizard and I'm not much of one. Why should it fall to us to fix this mess?"

Conryu smiled and closed his eye. "We have to do it because we're the only ones who can. You're right, I'd just as soon never cast another spell as long as I live, but I can't stand aside and let innocent people die if I can stop it. In the end, I'm a warrior and it's a warrior's responsibility to protect those who can't protect themselves. So my dad says anyway."

She sniffed. "You're braver than me. I just want to bury my head in the sand and pretend everything will be fine."

"Don't sell yourself short. You could have stayed behind with Maria, but you chose to come with me. That took guts and I appreciate it."

"You must tell her, Master."

"Quiet, Prime."

Kelsie wiped her eyes. "Tell me what?"

"Prime."

"I'm sorry, Master, but part of my task is to protect you. He's expending extra energy to keep you and his other friend safe. Before he retrieved you, Master eliminated the guardian beasts, casting two extra dark portal spells for no other reason than to spare your feelings."

"Is that true?"

Conryu sighed, mentally cursing his disobedient scholomantic. "Yes, it was safer for you if I dealt with the shadow beasts before I returned to collect you. I didn't think an extra spell or two would make this much difference. You and Jonny were so eager to help, I didn't have the heart to tell you."

Kelsie smacked him on the forehead. "You said you wouldn't lie to me."

"I didn't."

"You weren't completely honest."

"No, but I didn't keep any important secrets from you. If Loudmouth here hadn't spoken up you'd have never known."

"That's a thin line. No more, Conryu. If you need us to stay out of your way just say so. This is bigger than our feelings."

"Okay. Sorry."

* * *

Jonny left Conryu on the park bench looking gray and worn down. In all the years he'd known his best friend, Conryu had never looked as bad as he did today. Even when they both caught the flu after splashing through the river in the middle of winter five years ago and he had a fever of a hundred and three.

Maybe a good rest would set him to rights. Jonny didn't know much about magic or wizards. They only spoke about them at school to warn the regular soldiers to avoid them. Weaponized Humans, which was how the military referred to wizards like Conryu, were looked at the same way as tanks or jets. Any grunt stupid enough to take one on directly deserved to get squashed.

Jonny refused to think of Conryu as a weapon. That giant three-headed dog on the other hand... He shuddered. He reached the sidewalk and soon spotted a taxi. A piercing whistle got the driver's attention.

He climbed in and gave directions to the government plaza. The driver took off and he settled back in the seat. The cushions and springs had long since given out and he sunk in a foot. He planned to have the taxi stop outside the parking lot and make his way on foot.

It would be easy enough to find Conryu's mom's car, but he needed to go inside and talk to someone about what was happening to his friend. Maybe one of the other wizards would have an idea how to help him.

The ride took fifteen minutes. Jonny directed the driver to pull over half a block from the entrance. The cabbie looked back at him like he was nuts then shrugged and pulled to the side. Ten dollars lighter Jonny hopped out and set off for the plaza.

Since it was early afternoon on a Wednesday there shouldn't be any problem getting in. Dozens of people came and went all day every day. He carried the box under his arm like a courier and strode down the sidewalk and up the blacktop just like he had every right to be there.

The Department of Magic wasn't hard to spot what with the giant pentagram on the side. He stopped and looked from the magic building to the science building. He could hunt up the car, drop the box and let Maria know it was there in five minutes.

No, he needed to find some way to help his friend.

Jonny turned firmly toward the magic building and marched forward. He hadn't even reached the door before his hair started standing on end. Something was wrong. No one was coming or going. He figured the place would be buzzing like a kicked hornet's nest. Maybe everyone was busy trying to figure out what to do about the crazy wizards.

Inside the doors the entry area was abandoned. All the little cubby holes where the secretaries waited to greet visitors were empty. His footsteps echoed as he walked across the tile floor. Creepy.

He fished the phone out of his pocket and dialed Maria. "I'm in the lobby. Where are you? We need to talk. He isn't hurt, but I wouldn't say he was okay either. I'm on my way."

Jonny followed Maria's instructions, taking the elevator to the top floor and walking down the empty halls to her father's office. When he reached the door he hung up and pushed it open.

Maria ran over. "What's wrong?"

"I don't know. After we retrieved the box Conryu looked kind of gray and worn out. There wasn't a mark on him and we didn't have much of a fight, but he looked like he'd gone ten rounds in the cage."

"How many spells did he cast?" A woman in a gray robe made her way around the desk and relieved him of the box.

"I don't know, three or four of those black portal things, a couple others to clean the black gunk off your box and smash the gem inside. That's all I saw."

"Terra?" Maria switched her attention from him to the woman.

"Casting four portal spells in an hour would have me in the hospital for a week. The only way to recover from excessive casting is to rest. How long Conryu will need is impossible to say, but we know how long he has. It's extremely important you minimize his casting."

"Yeah. But we need some way to move around and if we can't go by portal..."

Maria's mom tossed him her keys. "Take my car. If I can contribute nothing else I can offer that."

Jonny snagged the keys. "Thanks. I'll be gentle with it."

"You'd better be." She smiled to show she wasn't serious.

"What's going on around here? This place is like a tomb. There's an emergency out there. We could use a little help."

Maria's dad offered a helpless shrug. "The mayor has placed us under house arrest, though it appears he isn't overly concerned about enforcing it. If we tried to leave the building it would probably be a different matter."

"I have to head back," Jonny said. "Wish us luck."

* * *

Lin didn't pay a great deal of attention when Conryu's friend delivered the box and gave an update on his condition. Whatever was happening on the magical end of this crisis was beyond his influence. After many years of experience, first in the military then the police department, he'd learned to move anything outside his control to the back of his mind and focus on the task at hand. And that task was figuring out who was in the conference room advising the mayor.

Whoever they were, they didn't appear to have existed two years ago. Since his police access code had never been revoked he could still use the department's files and research programs. One of them swept the web for any and all information about a given person.

Whoever created the woman's persona had done an excellent job for the past eighteen months, but beyond that they'd become lazy. Lin found a tidbit here, another clue there, obviously fake information planted to make it look like Maggie Chin had existed before a year and a half ago. There was enough to stand up to a cursory search, but if anyone really dug into her past it was clear the identity was a fraud.

Lin glanced up from his computer. Terra was absorbed in the remains of the artifact that Conryu had found. Maria was pacing again while her mother tried to massage some of the tension out of her husband's shoulders. Master Sho sat with his back straight, eyes closed, and breathing even. Lin recognized the simple meditative pose. Sensei had to be worried about his son, but like Lin he'd learned to control himself.

He hated to put more stress on his already careworn supervisor, but Chief Kane needed to know what he'd discovered. "Sir? It appears the mayor's advisor isn't who she claims to be."

Chief Kane patted his wife's hand, got up, and walked around the desk to look at Lin's computer. "Show me what you've found."

"As far as I can tell Maggie Chin didn't exist before a year and a half ago. Do you know who handles background checks for the Department in Central?"

"The security department, same as here. I have no idea which individual is responsible or even if it's just one person."

"Okay. Do we need to let the mayor know his advisor is a fraud?"

Chief Kane scratched his head. "Yes, but without proof of who she actually is he may not believe us given our status. Did you find anything that proves she's not who she claims to be?"

"No, sir. It's a lot of little things that add up to a big thing. I can make the case, but it's not going to be written in flashing neon."

"What about the man?"

"Without his name I can't even begin to start a search."

"How about a picture?"

Lin nodded. "I can work with that."

"Scoot over."

Lin moved aside and watched as Chief Kane accessed the security camera footage. It took most of five minutes, but he rewound to when the mayor arrived. Next they went super slow-motion until the man looked up. "Gotcha, whoever you are."

Lin resumed his seat and took a screen capture of the image. He ran the scanning program and in short order came up with a match. "Uh-oh."

"What is it?" The chief looked over his shoulder.

"Apparently our mystery man is a model. I found about twenty images of him on a stock photo website."

"I seriously doubt he's moonlighting as a male model. Terra, did you notice anything magical about the male advisor?"

Terra looked up from the box. "I didn't even think to check him. Basing an illusion on a photograph isn't unusual."

Chief Kane straightened up. "Ladies and gentlemen, I think we have a serious problem."

* * *

Even from a distance it was clear to Jonny that Conryu had regained some of his strength. He was sitting up and the ashen look to his skin had gone away. That was a relief. Nothing like resting on a hot girl's lap to set a man to rights. He needed to find one of his own. It wasn't fair that Conryu had two girlfriends and he didn't even have one.

He pulled up beside the park, rolled down the window, and blew a sharp whistle. When they looked his way he waved. Conryu and Kelsie hurried over and climbed in, him in the front and her in the back.

"Did you steal Mrs. Kane's car?" Conryu asked.

"No." Jonny pointed at the keys dangling from the ignition. "She loaned it to me with the admonition not to damage it. I also received strict instructions that you're not supposed to use any more magic than absolutely necessary. So where to?"

"Pendal's Funeral Home. I can't remember the address."

"No sweat. This baby has a state-of-the-art computer." Jonny fiddled with the touch screen in the dash, typed in the name of the funeral home and a minute later they were on their way.

He drove carefully, never breaking the speed limit or ignoring even minor traffic laws. The last thing they could afford was to get pulled over by the cops. By now every officer in the city probably knew what Conryu looked like and that he was wanted. It would be interesting to see what crime they were claiming he'd committed.

Despite the fact that he dressed like a delinquent and liked to ride a bike, Conryu had never been in serious trouble in his life. If anything, Conryu was the sort of person that would keep others from getting into trouble. He'd steered Jonny clear of a problem or two over the years.

Jonny darted a look at his best friend. Conryu held that creepy book to his chest like he was afraid someone might want to steal it. As if there was a huge market for talking, demon-faced books that could fly. Jonny wouldn't have taken the thing if offered it for free.

From the back seat Kelsie said, "Isn't it strange? Everyone's going about their business just like there was no danger of the city being attacked at the end of the day."

"Never underestimate the power of denial," Conryu said. "Look at me. A year ago I would have denied the possibility of even being a wizard. Now here I am running around trying to save a city that wants to kill me to protect themselves and using a ton of magic to do it. My protests to the contrary didn't make much impact on reality."

Jonny winced. Talk about bitter. He'd never heard Conryu say anything like that.

They rolled up and parked behind a white hearse. "What now?" Jonny asked.

"Now I portal in, track down the second box, and deal with whatever protections are waiting."

"Cool." Jonny unbuckled his seatbelt and reached for the door.

"We'll wait here," Kelsie said.

"What?" Jonny must have misunderstood. "We can't just sit here."

"Conryu will need to expend extra power to protect us. It'll be safer for everyone if we stay behind and keep watch on the funeral home. Does this model have a built-in phone?"

Jonny tapped the touchscreen. "Yeah."

"Conryu can just call us to pick him up when it's done."

"I'll be quick." Conryu slid out of the car and chanted in that weird language that made Jonny's skin crawl just listening to it.

One of those black disks appeared and he was gone.

Jonny twisted around and stared at Kelsie. "What's the idea? We're supposed to be helping him."

Her pretty lips gave a sad twist. "We are helping him. Staying out of Conryu's way is the best thing we can do. My magic is too weak to make a difference and you don't have any at all. Every bit of power he doesn't have to expend protecting us is that much more he'll have to fight with."

"He's my best friend. Just sitting here while he goes into danger makes me sick."

"I know. I love him too."

Chapter 5

The Second Box

Conryu left Jonny and Kelsie behind and entered the endless darkness of Hell. Cerberus appeared beside him and Conryu laid a hand on the demon dog's massive flank. Power flowed into him.

He looked up at Cerberus's panting heads. "Thanks."

Prime flew up out of his grasp. "That's part of a guardian demon's job, to protect you when you're weak. Or in this case to loan you a little extra power so you hopefully won't need protecting. It is good that you left the others behind. The girl understands and your other friend will as well."

"I hope you're right." Conryu turned his focus on Cerberus. "Okay, boy, time to hunt. Just like before."

Cerberus barked and began sniffing. It took a little longer this time as Conryu wasn't right at the site of the missing box, but soon enough Cerberus was running through the dark with Conryu on his back. Seconds passed before Cerberus pulled up and growled.

A little ways ahead of them a trio of raven-winged demons flew around a central point. The demons turned crimson eyes on them, but didn't attack.

"Corvus demons," Prime said. "Bound to protect that location. Our enemy has taken added precautions."

"How strong are they?" The demons had skinny arms and legs that ended in talons and emaciated bodies covered in thick feathers.

"Not overly, as demons go, but they're fast. Cerberus will have difficulty killing them. Fortunately, they're so weak they have no hope of causing him real harm. Under normal circumstances even a large group of Corvus demons would flee at Cerberus's approach. This lot has been bound so they have no choice but to fight."

"So it's a delaying tactic."

"Most likely, Master."

"Well, we don't have time to waste. Prime, keep your distance." He patted Cerberus. "Ready, boy?"

The growl deepened, vibrating Conryu's legs. He took that as a yes.

"Go!"

Cerberus lunged toward the demons, causing them to scatter. One swung wide and tried to come at them from the rear.

Conryu threw his hand out. "All things burn to ash, Inferno Blast!"

The stream of flames forced the Corvus to swing out wider. Cerberus raced after another of the demons, which beat its wings furiously to stay clear of three snapping jaws.

Another stream of fire forced the demon to flinch left. The sideways movement slowed it just enough for Cerberus's head on that side to bite down on its leg.

Cerberus gave a great shake and ripped the limb off. Reddish-black ichor gushed out as the demon spiraled down and out of sight, whether dead or dying Conryu didn't know.

They skidded to a stop and spun. Through the fight and wild movements Conryu never felt in danger of losing his seat on the demon dog's back. Some additional magic he didn't understand must have held him in place.

The Corvus demons came in from above, one to the left and one to the right, as they raced back toward the box's hiding place. Conryu raised both hands and pictured flames coming from them. "Inferno Blast!"

Twin streams of flame surged out. He missed the one on the left, but burned a wing off the one on the right. It spiraled out of control and disappeared into the darkness. That left one more. "After him, boy."

All three heads barked in unison as Cerberus put on a burst of speed. The terrified-looking Corvus tried to flee, but after a certain distance it was like it hit a wall and veered sharply right. For the second time, the turn did in their prey.

Cerberus snagged a wing with each of his outer heads and bit down on the demon's body with his central head. Several wet crunches later the remains of the Corvus vanished in a puff of noxious smoke.

Conryu scratched between the central head's ears. With Cerberus's help he'd only had to use a minimal amount of power. The demon dog groaned and padded over to the point where the trail ended. Conryu hopped off. "Good job, boy."

Prime flew over to join them. "You two fought well together."

"Thanks. Let's have a look at what we're dealing with this time. Grant me the power to see through realms, Vision Gate!"

The window into the mortal realm appeared in the darkness. An identical box sat on an identical pedestal in a very similar-looking stretch of sewer. He guided the window around the vicinity. There were six shadow beasts that resembled lions guarding this location along with a dead guy dressed like a biker.

"What do you make of him?" Conryu asked.

Cerberus growled and Prime said, "Just looking at it I'd say zombie, but why would anyone bother with adding such a weak creature to the mix? A single shadow beast would be more effective than a dozen zombies."

The three of them watched the odd collection of monsters for another minute as Conryu tried to think of a good way to deal with so many enemies. The shadow beasts didn't hold up at all well against his fire blasts, but he had no idea how tough the new monster was.

"Suggestions?" he asked.

"We don't have enough information, Master."

He shrugged. They'd just have to go in and do their best, the same as always. "Will Cloak of Darkness offer me any protection from the shadow beasts?"

"Yes, the creatures are basically pure magic given a sort of life. The spell should offer as much protection against them as against the fire cats you trained against."

"Should?"

"With magic nothing is certain."

"So I've noticed."

* * *

Terra closed the lid on the box. The material that remained of the artifact was fascinating. Her preliminary tests indicated it was crystalized necroplasma. How many lives had Mercia sacrificed to create her artifacts and their various protections? Not nearly as many as she intended to slaughter if the Society's demands weren't met, that was certain.

As horrible as it was to summon a horde of monsters and set them loose in the city, it somehow seemed even worse to intentionally murder someone and use their life force in a magical ritual. Maybe it was the personal nature of the act.

Orin was talking and Terra wrenched her focus back to the problem at hand.

"It's clear to me now that the people advising the mayor aren't who they claim to be," the chief said. "As I see it we have two choices: We can try to figure out who they are or we can challenge them directly and expose them in front of the mayor."

"I've done all I can as far as research goes," Lin said. "Our next move is to contact Central and talk to whoever handled the primary vetting."

Orin shook his head. "If the job was as sloppy as you say then whoever did it may be working with our imposters."

"If that's the case then our only recourse is confrontation," Lin said. "Where's Clair? I haven't seen her all day."

"She's locked up in her casting chamber meditating and trying to restore her magic." Terra shook her head. The poor woman was obsessed with getting her power back. Terra had tried to tell Clair that only time would set things right, but that didn't reassure the impatient wizard. "As she is now Clair would only be in the way."

"So it's just us?" Orin asked.

"We are not without resources." Terra met Shizuku's gaze and received a faint nod. "Two wizards along with Lin's magic gun are a potent combination. Besides, they only brought two guards."

"No sense wasting time." The chief started toward the door.

He only managed two steps before Shizuku laid a hand on his shoulder. "You and Maria should stay here. We'll return when it's safe."

"This is my responsibility," Orin said.

"Yes, dear, but if it comes to a fight it'll be better if we don't have to worry about the two of you." Shizuku turned to Conryu's father. "Sho, maybe you too—"

"These people are hunting my son. I will join you."

Terra had never been the fearful sort, but when she heard Sho Koda speak in that tone, a chill ran down her back. His expression never flickered, but if pure, cold rage had a sound it was Sho's voice.

Shizuku must have heard it too. "Alright, the four of us then."

Orin dug his access card out of his pocket and handed it to Shizuku. "This will open any door in the building. My lock code is our anniversary plus Maria's birth month. Be careful."

Shizuku kissed him and nodded. "We'll be back before you know it."

Terra wished she had someone to kiss goodbye. She glanced at Lin, but he was checking his weapon. Sho stood and led the way to the door. Terra had never seen anyone move that smoothly. He reminded her of a hunting cat, all power and balance.

Outside the office Terra assumed the lead, heading towards the stairs. The conference room was two floors below them. At the landing she opened the door a crack and peeked out. The two guards were standing on either side of the entrance.

She could take them out with magic easily enough, but if either of the imposters were disguised wizards they'd sense it. "There are two guards. No way we can sneak past them."

"I will deal with them." Sho slipped out into the hall, not giving her a chance to stop him.

He strode toward the guards, making no effort to conceal his approach, not that there was anywhere he could have hidden were he so inclined. As he moved closer, the nearest guard, a big, broad-shouldered man whose suit was at least one size too small, stepped away from the wall and raised his hand.

"You can't come any closer, sir. Please turn back now."

Sho darted in, grabbed the guard's extended hand, and twisted it. The joint locked. Sho stepped closer and drove his elbow into the side of the guard's head. He wouldn't have gone down any harder if he'd been hit with an ax.

The second guard went for his gun. The pistol came out just in time for Sho to grab the barrel and wrench it to the side. Terra heard his trigger finger snap from the stairwell. Sho jerked the pistol from the guard's maimed hand and cracked him upside the head with it, sending a second body to the floor.

Sho looked her way and motioned the group to join him in the hall.

* * *

Conryu conjured a pair of fire globes then opened the portal thirty yards up the tunnel from where the guardians congregated. That should give him time to react to whatever they did. The instant he emerged, four of the shadow lions charged straight at him while the other two ran the opposite way. The dead biker thing just stood beside the pedestal.

"All things burn to ash, Inferno Blast!" The flames streamed down the tunnel at the charging monsters. One was obliterated instantly. One got singed and the remaining two avoided any damage by leaping up and running along the ceiling.

He waved his hand back and forth, up and down, trying to burn them all away. This bunch was more nimble than the hounds and he only destroyed one more before they forced him to backpedal.

"By my will be bound, oh child of Hell. Your thoughts are my thoughts, your desires, my desires, Domination!"

The surviving shadow beasts shuddered as the spell settled over them.

"Stop!"

They went rigid. Conryu let out the breath he'd been holding.

"Master, the other two are coming from behind us."

Clever things. He focused his will on his bound servants. "Kill the approaching beasts."

The shadow lions fought him for a second, but his magic held. Baring black fangs they charged past him down the tunnel.

"Can shadow beasts actually destroy each other?"

"Your guess is as good as mine, Master. I've never heard of them fighting one another. Their hatred is reserved for the living. Rending shadowy flesh will give them no pleasure."

"Well let's at least hope they can keep the others busy. Somehow I think I'll need all my focus if I want to beat this new guy. Keep an eye on the kitties and let me know if they finish up before I do."

"Yes, Master."

Conryu left Prime to watch his back and eased closer to the box. When he was twenty feet away the undead biker shifted to block him. It leaned forward and for a moment Conryu hoped it was about to fall over.

It charged.

The hulking corpse ran faster than the shadow beasts. Only a lifetime of training allowed him to dodge a fist the size of a bowling ball. The punch skimmed by him and crashed into the tunnel wall, crushing a chunk out of the stone and sending gravel clattering against his face.

He ducked the backhand that took a piece out of the opposite wall. Conryu leapt away and focused on the exposed arm. "Shatter!"

The spell blew a hunk out of its bicep revealing a line of liquid darkness running down the middle of its arm. He'd expected the whole arm at least to disintegrate so that wasn't a good sign.

"Master, the body houses a nether spirit. It will be resistant to low-level magic."

Conryu did a backflip, narrowly avoiding a kick that would have crushed his chest. “I only know low-level spells for the most part. Shatter!”

His spell blew a fist-sized piece out of the undead’s thigh.

It raced forward, seeming unbothered by the injury, and landed a glancing blow that sent Conryu flying into the tunnel wall. He rolled aside an instant before a size-twenty boot came crashing down where his head had been a moment before.

Conryu scrambled to his feet and threw out a hand. “All things burn to ash, Inferno Blast!”

The stream of flame hit the undead square in the face. When the torrent stopped, its face had been burned down to the skull. The stench of roasted meat almost covered the sewer stink.

As with all his other attacks the monster seemed unperturbed by the damage. It opened its mouth and smoke emerged. A massive right cross came too fast for Conryu to dodge.

He managed a cross block, but it only minimized the impact. The blow still carried enough force to send Conryu sprawling and sliding through the filth that ran down the center of the tunnel. His forearms ached from the force of the blow, but at least his chest hadn’t been crushed.

“Master, I fear you’re not strong enough to defeat this enemy.”

Conryu was starting to fear that as well. Unfortunately he didn’t have any choice.

Wait, he did have a choice. He wasn’t strong enough to kill this thing, but he’d bet his bike Cerberus was.

He focused on the ground at the monster’s feet. “Reveal the way through infinite darkness. Open the path, Hell Portal!”

The black disk appeared directly under the guardian's feet. It fell most of the way through before its fingers caught the tunnel floor.

"Cerberus." Conryu focused all his wrath on the undead. "Kill!"

Like some unfortunate swimmer in a horror movie, the biker thing was dragged down into the dark. He doubted it would last five seconds against Cerberus. He willed the portal to close just in case it tried to escape.

"Master, the shadow beasts approach."

Conryu threw his hand up just as the first black lion came into view. "All things burn to ash, Inferno Blast!"

The beast was burned away in an instant. He adjusted his aim to sear the one running along the ceiling. It tried to drop to the floor, but he kept the flame on it until the creature burst into black mist.

"That's the last of them, Master."

Conryu closed his fist, ending the spell. In that moment he wanted nothing so much as to slump to the ground and sleep for a week. That wasn't a luxury he could afford just now.

He crossed his wrists and fingers. "Darkness dispels everything."

The basketball-sized sphere of dark magic blew away the wards and necroplasma protecting the box. Five steps closed the distance between Conryu and the pedestal. He placed both hands over the box. "Shatter!"

Splinters and shards of dark crystal went flying down the tunnel.

Conryu staggered over to the filthy tunnel wall and leaned against it. He barely had strength enough to raise his arm, but the thought of resting his face on whatever slime covered the stone gave him a boost of energy.

"Master, this is not a good place to recover. If our enemy sends more shadow beasts you'll have nowhere to hide."

"I know. Just give me a minute to get my wind back."

He closed his eyes and took slow, deep breaths, trying in vain to ignore the rank odor. It felt like the filth coated his tongue and the back of his throat. After a minute or two he started down the tunnel. Hopefully he'd find a manhole, along with the strength to open it.

* * *

Terra and the others joined Sho in the hall outside the conference room. She stepped over the body of the nearest guard and eyed the door. "Reveal."

No wards glowed in her enhanced vision. Maybe her initial impression had been correct and the advisors from Central were just ordinary liars. And maybe pigs could fly. Shizuku put her hands on Lin's and Sho's shoulders and murmured in Angelic. Both men lit up as the light magic shield sprang into place around them. Shizuku repeated the spell on herself.

She should cast a protective spell of her own, but fire magic wasn't subtle like light magic. If they marched in there and she was wearing a cloak of flames it might lead to a fight and right now Terra was more interested in talking.

Lin drew his pistol, but held it at his side out of sight. Shizuku nodded and Terra pushed the door open. The conference room was dark save for the light from a computer screen. The mayor sat in front of it, watching the feed from three different news channels. Terra flicked the light switch, but nothing happened.

Beside him the fake female advisor rested her hand on his back and whispered in his ear. A faint aura of magic leaked from between her fingers.

"She's a wizard," Terra said.

"Where's the guy?" Lin asked.

Shizuku raised her hands. "Let there be Light!"

Bright white orbs flew to every corner of the room. In the far corner a massively muscled creature in the tattered remains of a suit was hunched over a pair of mangled, partially consumed bodies. Bits of flesh dangled from its fangs. It was a demon of some sort and radiated dark magic.

Terra swallowed the lump in her throat. Whatever it was, it looked strong. When she'd led the group here she hadn't expected to confront a demon and a wizard.

The woman left the mayor's side and turned to face them. "You were told to remain in the executive office. Your services are not needed here."

Her words held the power of magic. They washed over Terra like a wave trying to force her out of the room. She clenched her jaw and focused her will. No one could control her unless she allowed it. After a few seconds that felt more like hours the spell faded and her mind cleared.

"You are strong willed, stronger than this weakling at least." She gave the mayor a casual swat across the back of the head. "Pity for you. If you had submitted this would have gone much easier for you."

Dark magic burst from the advisor. Maggie Chin vanished and a bat-winged female demon appeared. Exquisitely feminine with tiny horns on her forehead and a long, twitching tail, the succubus was stunning. Terra's heart raced and she wasn't even into that sort of thing.

Delicate white fingers grew six-inch black talons. From its place in the corner the second demon roared.

"Lin, you're with me. Shizuku, you and Sho handle the big one."

"Flames swirl and roar. Guard me from all enemies, Fire Armor!" Flames surrounded Terra from head to foot. It would take a potent attack to break her defense.

To her left a lightning bolt cracked. She spared the others a quick glance. Sho was racing to close with the demon while Shizuku blasted it with a second bolt.

They were on their own for now. The succubus sauntered around the table, hips swaying from side to side, only strategically placed black flames covering her nakedness.

"Are you certain you wouldn't rather surrender your will to me? I'm a generous mistress. I promise I won't even kill you when this business is settled."

"All things burn to ash, Inferno Blast!" Terra threw her hand forward and a torrent of flames streaked toward the demon.

A dark aura sprang up at once around her, parting the fire, and keeping it from burning her. Lin fired two shots, but both bullets exploded before impact.

"You'll have to do better than that." The succubus flicked her wrist and a black blade streaked toward Terra.

Lin tackled her and the blade flew over their heads. "We're out of our league," he whispered into her ear.

Terra was quickly coming to that conclusion as well, but she wasn't ready to give up yet. From the floor she chanted, "Flood the world with flames, Fire Surge!"

A rush of flames, twice as powerful as her first spell, poured from her cupped hands. They plowed into the succubus's dark barrier and forced the demon back one step, then another.

For half a second she imagined the spell might penetrate, then the flames guttered and died. Beyond them the demon remained unharmed.

"That was better." The succubus raised her hand and a ball of black energy gathered.

Lin raised his pistol and put three rounds into the ebony sphere. The dark magic devoured the bullets like they were nothing. If that spell hit them it would do exactly the same thing.

* * *

Sho had heard the reports of his son's battles with demons and other magical threats, but until this moment he hadn't fully appreciated what that meant. His roundhouse kick struck the red-skinned monster in the side of the jaw with enough force to break the neck of a normal man. The demon didn't flinch.

It opened its mouth so wide Sho thought its head might split in half. He jerked his leg back before the demon had a chance to bite his foot off. Sho ducked two slashes from taloned hands big enough to rip him in half.

He danced back and a third lightning bolt struck the demon in the chest. The red skin darkened, but beyond that the attack had no effect. He darted in again, landing a dozen machine-gun punches before leaping clear to avoid a backhand.

It was like punching a concrete pillar and every bit as effective. Only the demon's relative lack of speed kept Sho alive. His son had fought creatures like this and won. He had a whole new respect for what Conryu's magic could do.

Shizuku sent a lance of white energy crashing into the demon's chest, doing every bit as little damage as she had with the lightning. The demon took a step toward them and Sho took a step back.

This was pointless. If he pounded that thing until his fists broke it wouldn't accomplish anything. As a warrior Sho feared nothing, but he knew when he was in a fight he couldn't win and this was it.

He risked a glance over at the government wizard and Lin. They were lying on the floor with the female demon standing over them. The creature had a ball of energy in its hand.

An idea popped into his head. A foolish, desperate idea, but if ever there was a time for foolish desperation this was it. He sprinted across the room toward the female demon, ignoring Shizuku's confused look as he went past.

He'd covered most of the distance before the creature noticed him. It swung his way, doing half his work for him. He leapt and kicked at its head, missing intentionally.

The instant he landed Sho spun and kicked the wrist above the black ball, knocking it away from Lin and toward the other demon. He so startled the female that she released the ball.

It streaked toward her hulking companion, exploding on impact. The conference room shook. In the chaos Sho grabbed Lin and Terra and pulled them to their feet.

"We need to go," he said.

Terra nodded and muttered something in one of those nonsense languages the wizards used. A wall of fire sprang up between them and the demons. Shizuku had already reached the doors and was motioning for them to hurry as they ran.

The group darted out into the hall and Terra led them back toward the stairwell. Inside, they went down instead of up.

"We need to return for Orin and Maria," Shizuku said.

"No, we need to lead the demons away from them, not back." Terra took the steps two at a time.

"Would that blast have killed the male?" Sho couldn't imagine anything surviving an impact like that, but he also wouldn't have believed it could live through three lightning strikes, so he had little confidence in his theory.

"No, that orb was pure dark magic. It might have stunned the demon, but it wouldn't have done any real damage." Terra pulled up at the third-floor platform. "We need some extra firepower."

* * *

Kelsie really wanted to move around, but she didn't dare leave the car lest she draw unwanted attention. Conryu had been gone fifteen minutes already. Given that no time passed when he was in Hell that meant he'd been trying to deal with the box and its protections all this while. It had only taken him five minutes to handle the first one. Something must have gone wrong.

Had she made a mistake, not to insist on going with him? No, she knew what she was capable of and her feeble magic wouldn't even be enough to stop a single shadow beast. And Jonny couldn't do magic at all. If they'd gone they'd have only slowed him down. Nonetheless she wished she knew what was happening.

"Do you think he's okay?" Jonny asked, speaking her thoughts out loud.

"Conryu's the strongest wizard ever. If he can't handle this no one can." God, she wished she felt as confident as she sounded.

"He's only one man. No matter how strong he is, Conryu doesn't have eyes in the back of his head."

"He has Prime and Cerberus. I'm worried too, but we have to trust that he'll be okay."

Jonny twisted around and looked at her. "I swore to myself after that business at the carnival, when he put himself in danger to protect everyone, that if it ever happened again I wouldn't run. That I'd stand beside him and fight. Now here I am, just like last time, useless and waiting. What kind of friend am I that I let him face this alone?"

"The same kind as me, I suppose. While I wish with all my heart I could help, I know I can't. And neither can you. It isn't a matter of not caring, it's about knowing your limitations."

The car phone rang and Jonny spun back around. An icon of a handset was flashing on the screen. He touched it. "Conryu?"

"Yeah." He sounded so weak. "I'm at Seventh and Maple. There's a little cafe."

"Got it. We're on our way." The line went dead and Jonny shook his head. "He sounded worse than last time."

"Must have been a harder fight. That can't be a surprise after he destroyed the first box." Kelsie glanced at the time. Twelve hours to go.

Jonny pulled out and made his way through the busy streets. She wasn't familiar with Sentinel City, but Jonny seemed to know right where he was going. Five minutes later she spotted the cafe and Conryu, sitting slumped at one of the tables. He looked asleep.

Jonny double-parked right across from him, leapt out, and helped him back to the car. Several cars behind them honked, but they paid no attention. Conryu fell into the back seat beside her, Prime clutched in his grasp.

When he blinked and looked up at her his eyes were so red she expected blood to run down his cheeks. And what in heaven's name did he have on his clothes? The stink filled the car. Jonny got in behind the wheel and took off.

"Was it bad?" Kelsie adjusted his head so it rested on her lap. She murmured the cleaning spell in hopes of getting whatever the mess was off him.

"Demons, shadow beasts, and this weird zombie thing that almost took my head off. It's good you two didn't try and come with me. It was all I could do to protect myself."

"Where we headed?" Jonny asked.

"Nowhere for a while." Conryu tried to sit up but she pulled him back down. "Find a parking lot or something. I need to rest for a couple hours."

"One port in the storm coming up."

"Is two hours going to be enough?" Kelsie stroked his hair. The spell had cleaned the worst of the crud off his clothes and the seat. The mess now sat in a pile on the floor.

"We have three boxes to go. I don't dare take any longer."

Prime worked himself free from Conryu's grasp. "If you keep this pace up you'll kill yourself, Master. You need at least six hours' rest or a direct infusion of life energy."

“Six hours is out of the question,” Conryu said. “What about the second one?”

“There’s a spell, it’s actually a variation of Reaper’s Gale, that drains your target’s life force, but instead of dissipating it draws it into your body. It’s another one you’ll need to be careful with. Drain too much and your target dies.”

“Great, show me. I don’t know if I’ll use it, but it never hurts to be prepared. I need a spell that will make it easier to kill those zombie things too.”

While Conryu studied the book Kelsie studied him. He looked pale and weak, but the determination in his gaze never wavered. She knew he wouldn’t give up while he had breath in his body. She’d make sure he kept breathing, even if it killed her.

Chapter 6

Reaction

Lady Raven snapped her fingers and the image on her viewing mirror vanished. She understood everything now. It was clear from the moment he stepped out of the dark portal. Conryu was somehow tracing the path her boxes took through Hell.

How was he doing it? She knew of no spell that created such an effect. Regardless, he was doing it and in the process slowly destroying years of work along with her hopes for a long life as a Hierarch in the Society.

The defenses she'd put in place at the last location were the strongest possible given the time she had. She'd increased the number of shadow beasts at the remaining locations, but refused to sacrifice any more of her Faceless Ones. Galling as it was, she had to admit mere shadow beasts wouldn't be enough to hold the abomination off.

Lady Raven reached for her mask. If the mission was to succeed she needed to ask for help.

With her mask in place she stepped into the circle and cast the calling spell. The others had to be waiting near their own casting chambers. With the time of activation so close they'd want to be available in case of emergencies.

Well, this certainly qualified as one. It took less than a minute for the room to go hazy. The first to appear was Lady Wolf. Lady Tiger and Lady Dragon appeared shortly after that.

"What has happened?" Lady Dragon asked.

"The abomination has interfered and destroyed two of the artifacts."

The weight of Lady Dragon's regard pressed down on her. The anger and disappointment in her gaze burned Lady Raven's skin.

"I thought you put protections in place," Lady Wolf said.

"I did and I increased them after his first success." Lady Raven took a deep breath. "They were inadequate. I acknowledge that. If the mission is to have any hope of success I'll need help."

"We have no magic to offer you." Lady Dragon slapped the Scepter of Morgana against her palm.

"What about our other agents in the city? They were supposed to be helping capture the abomination."

"Yes, well, you're not our only disappointment today. Rennet has also been a spectacular failure with regards to capturing him. Apparently the police can't arrest someone they can't find."

Lady Raven couldn't suppress a faint smile. "If you can put me in contact with her I believe I can solve both our problems. And if I may add, perhaps elimination would be better than capture."

"Approved." Lady Dragon rattled off a phone number. "You can reach Rennet at that number. Be certain to tell her this is the last chance for both of you."

The Hierarchs vanished and Lady Raven found herself back in her casting chamber. She took off her mask and scrambled to reach her cellphone before she forgot the number Lady Dragon gave. Somehow she doubted it would be repeated if she asked.

* * *

Maria sat beside her father and stared at the laptop screen. He'd tapped into the building security cameras, allowing them to watch the others confront the imposters. Her heart had skipped a beat when the woman turned into a demon. Everyone had fought bravely, but in the end they'd been forced to flee.

Dad tapped a key, opening multiple windows in the screen. One showed Mom and her companions running down the stairwell, another stayed on the conference room. The male demon shook off the effects of his partner's blast and went after them. It crushed one of the unconscious guards' heads before turning down the stairs. Maria shuddered and looked away.

"Clever Terra," Dad muttered.

Maria looked back. "What's she doing?"

"Terra led them to the magical artifact storage room. There are plenty of things in there that will give them an edge over that monster."

"What's the other one doing?" Maria pointed at the window showing the conference room. The female demon had moved toward the door and stepped out into the hall.

Dad tapped another key and the view shifted. The demon headed for the stairs, but turned up instead of down.

"Uh-oh. Looks like we're going to have company." Dad closed the lid on the laptop and handed it to her. "Time to make ourselves scarce."

"Where are we going to go?" Maria's heart raced. She didn't know a single spell that would even make that thing blink if it came to a fight.

"Don't worry, sweetheart." Dad walked over to the left side of his office and groped around a blank section of wall. There was a click and a secret door slid aside. "Come on."

She slipped in ahead of him and a light came on overhead. A narrow corridor extended as far as she could see behind the wall. Dad joined her and secured the door.

"I didn't know this was here."

"Only the station chief knows about it. The old chief told me when I took over. No one has ever used it since the building was constructed. It was a fine tradition I had hoped to follow. These passages run all through the building. The idea was to have a way to escape and counterattack if the Department was ever assaulted."

"I don't know about counterattacking, but escape sounds good."

He took her hand and squeezed.

Out in the office an explosion was followed by crunching footsteps. Dad held a finger to his lips and nodded his head toward the far end of the passage. Maria tiptoed away from the door.

"I can smell you, mortals. Wherever you're hiding, I'll find you."

Nothing that evil should have such a beautiful voice. The demon could have been a professional singer. Maria choked off a hysterical giggle when she imagined the monster on one of the popular singing competitions. She had to focus.

"Hurry," Dad whispered. "There's a right turn just a little ways further then a ladder down."

She made the turn a moment before another explosion sounded behind them. Dad urged her on and Maria broke into a trot. If the demon had found the hidden passage there was no point in keeping quiet.

"So we have rats in the walls." The demon's voice echoed through the passage. "Good thing the exterminator's here."

Maria tried to swallow, but her throat was too dry. The ladder was just ahead. If they put some distance between themselves and their hunter, maybe they had a chance of escaping. She put her foot on the first rung and clambered down. Aside from a slight vibration the ladder was secure.

She made it to a small chamber at the bottom. There didn't appear to be an exit.

Her breath came in ragged gasps as she scrambled around for an exit. There had to be one. Dad wouldn't have led them to a dead end.

Dad hit the floor beside her and went directly to a section of wall no different from any other. He pressed a particular spot and a panel slid up revealing a number pad. When he input the code another door slid open.

She darted through it and he joined her a moment later. Another long hall greeted them. They'd barely taken a step when something heavy landed in the now-empty chamber. Maria froze, terror gripping her heart. It was a magical effect, her rational mind recognized that, but her primitive mind screamed at her not to move. If she held still maybe the monster wouldn't see her.

The muffled ring of a cellphone broke the spell. It was clearly coming from the other side of the door. What she couldn't understand was why a demon would have a phone in the first place and where the naked creature kept it.

"I'm a little busy right now." Maria heard the demon just as plain as day.

Silence, followed by, "Are you certain? Hold on. No, I don't want to disappoint Lady Dragon."

More silence.

"Very well. My rat problem will keep for the moment."

The clang of the demon's feet on the ladder climbing back up out of the hole set Maria free. She leaned against the wall and tried to calm her still-racing heart.

Dad rubbed her back. "Are you okay?"

"Yeah. What was that about and who's Lady Dragon?"

"I couldn't tell anything from the demon's side of the conversation, but Lady Dragon is the leader of the Le Fay Society. She's the one that delivered the ultimatum this morning. No one knows her true identity. If you're up to it we need to move."

Maria pushed away from the wall and took a step down the hall. Ahead of them a panel clattered open.

She took a step back before Angus's white-haired head popped into view. "Thank god. I was beginning to think I'd never find a way out of these cursed passages."

* * *

Conryu draped his arm across his eyes and tried to sleep. The back seat of a car wasn't the best place in the world to rest. His knees were almost touching his chin, the seatbelt was digging into his hip, and the sewer stink still lay over everything. Assuming they lived through the next day Conryu was going to have to spring for an auto detailing for Mrs. Kane. At least Kelsie's lap made a good pillow.

The car stopped and he looked out the window. Nothing but concrete walls and a pillar filled his vision. "Where are we?"

"Parking garage." Jonny switched the car off. "Figured it would be more out of the way than an open lot. Anything I can do?"

Conryu covered his eyes again. "Not right now. Once I get my strength back we need to go to St. Sara's Cemetery."

"No sweat, bro. Just say when."

Conryu raised his fist and Jonny gave it a bump.

He didn't think he actually slept, it was more a half-awake sort of thing. Conryu's mind wandered, trying to make sense of the situation he found himself in. Sometimes it felt like only days ago when the government wizard told him he had wizard potential and other times it felt like a whole different life.

"Master, I sense many people approaching."

"Probably shoppers returning to their cars." Jonny yawned. "There's a mall connected to this garage."

A gunshot rang out and a bullet slammed into the car. Conryu sat up, a blast of adrenaline washing away his exhaustion.

More shots clattered against the door and windshield. Ten guys with machine guns and bulletproof vests were advancing up the ramp toward them.

"How the hell did they find us?" Jonny had slid over into the passenger's seat and hunkered down amidst shards of the window.

"Beats me, but we can't stay here. Kelsie, scoot out the door. Careful not to expose yourself."

She opened the door and slipped out. Conryu crawled across the seat and dropped to the ground. Jonny joined them a moment later. "What now?" he asked.

Conryu flinched as a bullet ricocheted a little too close for comfort. "I was hoping you'd have a suggestion. You're the soldier."

"Sorry, dude. Soldiers have guns and armor. I'm a civilian today."

"Master, this may prove to be a fortuitous turn of events." Prime floated inches off the floor.

"What?" Kelsie's voice had turned shrill with fear.

"Those men will provide you with an excellent source of life energy. You can put them out of commission and restore yourself at the same time."

He wasn't thrilled about the thought of draining the life out of anyone. Another burst of gunfire made him duck. He wasn't thrilled about getting shot either.

Jonny lay on the ground and looked under the car. "They're almost on us. Five seconds and we'll be surrounded."

Kelsie clutched his arm. "Conryu."

This was no time to be squeamish. He eased free of Kelsie's grip and focused. He wanted to drain the police enough to knock them out, not kill them. "Fingers of the Reaper, black and twisted. Reach for my enemies and claw the life from them. Feed me their souls that I may be strong, Reaper's Grasp!"

A wailing moan filled the air and black spirits exploded from Conryu. The nearest cop came around the car just in time to have a formless cloud of darkness pass through his body.

The cop collapsed, twitching, to the concrete. Beyond the car the frightened cries mingled with the spirits' moaning. Full auto sprays of gunfire went off seemingly at random.

He sensed the first spirit returning before he saw it. The apparition slid through the car door like smoke and slipped into his chest. First cold then heat assaulted him. He stiffened as one after another of the spirits entered his body.

Weakness was burned away and a power unlike anything he'd ever experienced filled him to bursting. When the final bit of energy entered him he gasped and leaned forward. "What a rush."

Jonny peeked over the hood. "I don't see anything moving. I think we're good for now."

Conryu pulled himself to his feet using the bullet-riddled car for leverage. He glanced at the collapsed officer. The man's face was ghost white, but he was breathing which was more than they were willing to allow Conryu.

He helped Kelsie to her feet. When she looked over the car roof at the bodies sprawled across the pavement she buried her face in his chest. He held her for a moment then stepped back. "It's okay. I didn't kill any of them."

Jonny cleared his throat. "I don't think we should hang around here."

"Good call. Think you can find us a car?"

Jonny grinned. "No problem."

While Jonny went car shopping Conryu sat on the hood of their current ride. Prime flew up beside him. "Are you well, Master?"

"Better than that. I'm so buzzed I think I could tear that zombie thing apart with my bare hands."

"That's a side effect of this particular spell. It's also highly addictive. More than one dark wizard has fallen from the righteous path on a quest for ever more life energy. I wouldn't recommend using it more than necessary."

Jonny pulled up in a beat-up blue coupe that looked older than Conryu. "Jump in."

Conryu grabbed the handle and gave it a yank. It came free in his hand. Jonny leaned across and opened it from the inside. It was so tight Kelsie practically had to sit in his lap.

"Is this the best you could do?"

"Give me a break. All the new cars have antitheft devices. This was the only one I could hot-wire. Beats walking, right?"

"Barely."

Jonny shot him a middle finger and took off. They hadn't gone a hundred yards when they found a heavy truck with police emblems on the side blocking their way.

"Think they left the keys in it?" Conryu asked.

"I'll check." Kelsie hopped out and ran over to the truck. A few seconds later she was back. "No dice."

"Looks like we're walking after all." Jonny reached down to untwist the wires.

"Wait." Conryu focused on the ground under the truck. "Reveal the way through infinite darkness. Open the path, Hell Portal!"

The familiar black disk appeared under the front half of the truck. It teetered and fell in. The instant the rear end fell out of sight the portal snapped shut.

Jonny grinned and they bumped fists. Conryu turned to Prime as Jonny drove off. "The demons won't get mad if I drop a truck in their realm, will they?"

"Hell is infinite, Master. The vehicle is a speck in an endless ocean. I doubt anyone will even notice it."

Conryu hoped so. The fine for littering in Hell was probably stiff.

Chapter 7

Demons at the Department

Terra stopped in front of the sealed storage room door and panted for breath. It had been a long run and she wasn't as young as she used to be. At first she'd been concerned that the imposters had ordered everyone home early, now the empty halls came as a relief. The only way this could be worse was if she had to worry about the staff getting caught in the crossfire.

Shizuku stared back the way they'd come. Terra sensed no pursuit, but the light magic user was more sensitive to dark magic than her. "Anything?"

"It's faint but getting closer. The male is definitely on our trail."

Terra swallowed a curse, placed her hand on the metal plate beside the door and spoke the release spell. The door popped open revealing shelf upon shelf covered in magical artifacts.

"What is this place?" Sho asked.

"Storage. We keep potentially dangerous or valuable magical items here." She went in and soon came up with the

Flame Fist Gauntlet. "This, for instance, will increase my fire magic a great deal."

The gauntlet was still sized for the biker that had last worn it. Terra slipped it on and like all magical items it altered itself to fit her hand as if it had been made for her.

"Anything in there for light magic?" Shizuku asked.

Terra rummaged around, looking for the crystal amulet they'd brought in last year. She knew it was here somewhere.

Behind her Shizuku said, "Hurry, Terra, it's coming."

Her search grew more frantic. Where was it? Something flashed in one of the bins. There! The clear crystal amulet had sunk to the bottom of the container. She fished it out and stepped into the hall.

"Here." Terra handed the artifact to Shizuku who slipped it over her neck. The demon was so close now Terra sensed it even with her limited awareness of dark magic.

"This is a potent item." Shizuku fingered the central gem.

"Yeah, if we live through this I'll tell you the story of how we ended up with it. Lin, Sho, stay behind us." When the men had moved a safe distance back she said, "You bind it and I'll burn the bastard to the ground."

Shizuku nodded and raised her hands. The heavy thumps of the demon's tread vibrated the floor. It rounded the corner, its head brushing the ceiling. Had it gotten bigger? Muscles rippled under red skin stretched so tight it looked like it might tear.

Shizuku chanted in Angelic. Light gathered around the amulet and when she finished, the light released. White portals appeared all around the demon and golden chains shot out, wrapping up its arms, legs, and neck.

It thrashed and roared, snapping one of the chains immediately. Shizuku gestured and a new chain shot out to replace the broken one.

Terra clenched her gauntlet-covered hand. "Flames of deepest earth consume all things in your path. Flames of creation and flames of destruction rise and devour, Volcanic Core!"

She opened her hand and thrust it toward the ceiling. The floor trembled and tore open under the demon's feet. White-hot flames spewed forth, hiding the demon from view. Terra squinted, but her focus never wavered. Deep in the heart of the inferno a dark figure struggled.

The demon pressed through the flames, breaking more chains as it went. It was going to escape and if it did they'd never stop it before it tore them all to pieces.

The steel beams her spell exposed twisted and wrapped around the demon, keeping it from moving beyond the fire. Shizuku sent still more chains. Despite all that it continued to struggle to free itself.

Terra focused her will on the gauntlet and demanded it give more power. She had to end it now. The flames intensified until she couldn't even make out the shadow of the demon.

The floor above came crashing down, smashing through their floor and continuing on until the debris hit the lobby. Terra ended the spell. Nothing of the demon remained.

On the opposite side of the hole she'd burned in the floor stood Clair who, despite the danger, wore a huge grin. Terra understood completely. The moment the metal twisted she'd known Clair had regained her magic. For a wizard there was no greater joy.

"Excellent timing." Terra blew out a sigh and started to pull the gauntlet off.

Lin laid a hand on her shoulder. "You should keep that until we deal with the one upstairs."

The one upstairs. For half a minute she'd forgotten the succubus. She tugged the gauntlet back on tight. Dealing with that one would be tricky since it was holding the mayor hostage. She certainly wouldn't be able to use Volcanic Core on her.

"Maybe you'd better fill me in," Clair said.

"We'll talk as we walk. I need to check on Orin and Maria." Shizuku made no move to take off her borrowed amulet.

It went against protocol to let her keep using it, but under the circumstances Terra figured it was the best option. "Let's go."

* * *

Maria's heart about stopped when Angus's head appeared in the passage. She was starting to think she really wasn't cut out for adventure. A quiet little business far away from anything anyone would ever want to hold hostage sounded really good right now. She brushed a cobweb aside and did her best to ignore the musty, stale air.

"Angus." Her father had assumed the lead since he was the only one that knew his way around the passages. "How did you get in here?"

"I found the hidden access one day quite by accident when I stumbled against the wall and it slid open. Imagine my surprise. I had no idea the Department building even had hidden paths. I never did anything about it, but after I called Conryu it occurred to me that making myself scarce would be a prudent decision. I retreated to my office and entered the passages whereupon I got utterly lost."

"Don't feel too bad. I spent the better part of three weeks memorizing the layout of these passages. They're designed in an intentionally haphazard way to make it hard for those not familiar with them."

"I'll happily attest to their effectiveness. By the way, how is Conryu?"

"Okay as of a couple hours ago," Maria said. "He's disabled at least one of the artifacts and most likely a second by now."

Angus shook his head, sending white hair waving in every direction. "The boy's a marvel. Just imagine, after he saves the city he'll be even more famous. A true hero in every sense of the word, just like Merlin."

Maria wanted to slap him for bringing up his pet theory even when they were running for their lives. The last thing Conryu wanted was to be more famous. He was only doing this because no one else could.

An explosion sent dust raining down on her. "Dad?"

"Sounds like your mother and the others are back at it. Let's pick up the pace. I don't want to be in here if something collapses."

"Like what?" Angus's question came out as more of a croak.

"Like the building."

"What?" Angus staggered against the wall when another blast shook the floor.

Maria knew enough about the design of the Department's wards to know the odds of the whole building coming down on their heads was vanishingly small. She allowed herself a small smile. It was good that her father could still tease Angus, even in these circumstances. For some reason that, more than anything, made her believe they had a better chance to win this than they probably did.

They went down another floor before Dad finally led them to an exit. They stepped out into an office filled with books and papers. A green-and-red tartan hung on the wall above a cluttered desk.

"You found my office." Angus rushed over to his chair, slumped into it, and let out a groan. "God, that feels good. I was afraid if I didn't get off my feet soon I was going to faint."

The two guest chairs were filled with notebooks and papers. Maria cleared them off so she and her father would have a place to sit. "What are we going to do now?"

"That depends on Terra and your mother." Dad took the laptop and opened it. He searched through the various camera feeds until a smoke-filled image filled the screen. "Uh-oh."

A huge hole had been blown in the floor. There was no sign of Mom or the others, but there weren't any bodies either. That was something.

"They won't know where to find us."

Dad waved a hand. "They have a pair of skilled wizards with them and the three of us, along with the mayor and Clair, are the only humans in the building. I suspect they'll be along shortly."

* * *

The high from the infusion of life energy had faded to a faint buzz. As fantastic as it felt, Conryu was glad to return to normal. The giddy rush left him feeling invincible and that was a good way to do something stupid. He couldn't afford any mistakes. They only had nine hours left.

Jonny stopped and pulled over to the side of the road, dragging Conryu from his contemplations. Ten cop cars surrounded the cemetery and heavily armed officers patrolled the perimeter. There was no way to sneak through and Conryu wasn't eager to lay out more cops. They were supposed to be on the same side after all.

"What now, dude?"

"Reveal." Conryu squinted at the crumbling mausoleum where the box had been hidden during the winter. Dark wards crackled around it and the aura of one of the boxes was just visible through the walls. "She moved them back."

"What?" Kelsie turned to look at him.

"She moved the boxes back to their original hiding places, this one at least. It's smart; now her artifacts are protected by people I don't want to hurt instead of monsters I'd be happy to destroy."

"Or perhaps both," Prime said. "Shadow beasts could be hidden inside the crypt as a second line of defense. Mingling with the living would make them more difficult targets for you."

Conryu canceled the seeing spell. "Let's try the culvert. If they have that one on lockdown as well we can assume the police are working with the Le Fay Society and not against them."

Jonny did a U-turn, drawing several annoyed honks which he ignored. As they roared down the street Kelsie asked, "Couldn't you just portal in, deal with the box, and escape without the police noticing?"

"Maybe, but what if something goes wrong and I need to retreat? Having twenty plus machine guns pointing my way isn't very appealing. I wish I'd thought to borrow Mrs. Kane's ring when I got home from school."

"Why, what does it do?"

"She said it stopped bullets."

Kelsie chewed her lip and nodded. "That would certainly be handy."

It took almost half an hour to drive across town through the afternoon traffic. Jonny didn't even bother pulling down the street leading to the culvert. The police cars were visible from where he stopped.

"Goddamn it!" Conryu slammed his fist into the car door.

Wasn't it enough to have to deal with wards, shadow beasts, and demons? Now he had a bunch of cops who should be out evacuating people in the danger zone standing between him and the very things that put those people in jeopardy. It was a bad joke.

Conryu dug out the phone, flipped it open, and dialed Maria. She answered after the third ring. A stream of worries slammed into his ear and he held the phone away.

"Maria. Maria! I'm fine, really. Is your dad there? I need to talk to him. No, I'm not trying to get out of talking to you, I'm in a bit of a situation here and I need some advice. Please?"

A couple seconds later Mr. Kane came on. "Conryu, what's the problem?"

"The problem is a bunch of cops that are trying to stop me from getting to the boxes. A SWAT team damn near shot me twenty minutes ago, and the less said about Mrs. Kane's car the better. I need the police out of the way if I'm going to do my job. I can take them out if there's no other option, but the only spell I know that'll do it might kill everyone if I make a tiny mistake."

The silence stretched until it grew uncomfortable. "We have a bit of a situation here as well."

Mr. Kane filled him in on their demon problem. As he talked a headache built behind Conryu's eyes.

Mr. Kane added, "So the mayor has the police convinced you're the primary threat and they've deployed accordingly. Until we deal with the demon controlling him there's no way we can convince the police to back down and even then they might think it's a trick."

"I assume you have a plan."

"No. Terra and Shizuku think they can kill the creature, but there's every possibility of the mayor getting burned in the crossfire. I'm not sure that's a chance we can take."

"What if I come and use Domination to force her to release the mayor and return to Hell? It's that or I risk killing the police between me and the boxes. That's not a decision I'm comfortable making on my own."

"Alright, take the stairs up to the fourteenth floor. After Terra destroyed the second and third floors the elevators aren't working."

"Great. I thought your office was on the sixteenth floor?"

"It is, but we were forced to escape. We're working out of Angus's office for the moment."

Conryu groaned. A demon and the professor, fantastic.

* * *

Smoke was pouring out of the second-floor window when the car pulled into the Department parking lot. Why there weren't people pouring out of the other nearby government buildings was beyond Conryu. The lack of fire trucks was another mystery. There was a station three blocks north. They should have spotted the smoke from their front door.

The almost-empty parking lot gave them ample options, but Jonny parked as far from the doors as possible. Probably a good idea. If Conryu failed to keep the demon under control and it became a fight, well, better to have their ride a safe distance away.

They piled out of the car and Jonny looked around the empty lot. "You'd think it was a holiday."

"Yeah, Demon Apocalypse Day. Come on." Conryu led the way to the front doors.

When he pushed them open they found a heap of rubble in the lobby. The secretaries' desks were crushed under tons of steel and concrete. A haze of dust filled the air. Conryu covered his face and made his way around the debris and over to the stairwell.

The path was clear and he quickstepped it up to the fourteenth flour. By the time they reached the door Kelsie was gasping and Conryu's pulse raced. Only Jonny appeared unfazed. All that training must have paid off.

When Kelsie had stopped wheezing like a bellows with a hole in it, Jonny pushed the door open and they stepped out into an empty, undamaged hall.

"Shit! I forgot to ask which office belonged to Angus." Conryu pulled out the phone and dialed. "Hey, we're here. Which office is Angus's?"

Three doors to their left a door opened and Maria poked her head out. "This one."

She stepped into the hall and leapt into his arms the minute he came within reach. They shared a kiss and Conryu sighed. "I missed you. Though I'll admit I'm just as glad you weren't with me for the last two fights."

"Bad, huh?" She took his hand and led the group into Angus's office.

The professor was behind his desk, chin on chest, sound asleep. Thank god for small favors. Everyone else was sitting, standing, or leaning as was their preference.

"Hey, Dad."

His father nodded, but made no comment.

"Conryu," Mr. Kane said. "We're in a real mess here. That creature has complete control of the mayor and it's standing right next to him. Any offensive move will hurt him as much or more than her."

"Can you show me?"

Lin had a computer on his lap which he spun so Conryu could see the screen. There was an image of a room with a long table. Seated at the end of it in front of a computer with two monitors was a man in a suit and beside him was a pale, bat-winged demon. Both of them faced away from the camera, but from the curve of her hips it was clear the demon was a succubus. It might even be someone the Dark Lady knew.

He didn't expect that to help him any. From what she'd said it didn't seem like the Dark Lady got along especially well with others of her kind. Of course, if she'd gotten as strong as she claimed since becoming his agent, maybe he could use her as a threat against this succubus.

"So is there a plan?" Conryu asked. "Or do you just want to march up there and see what happens?"

When the silence had stretched to a breaking point he looked from Mr. Kane to Terra to Mrs. Kane before sighing. "Right. Let's go. Kelsie, stay close and be ready to put your hand on my back. A little power boost might be the difference between success and failure."

Maria glared and Kelsie beamed, walking right beside him as they left Angus's office. The old professor had slept through the whole discussion.

It was a short walk up to the next floor. When they stepped out of the stairwell Conryu grimaced. Two bodies lay on the floor, one of them with his head crushed flat, a pool of blood spreading around him.

"Looks like the demon wasn't careful where he stepped," Terra said.

Kelsie grabbed his arm and buried her face in his shoulder. He could almost feel Maria's gaze boring a hole through his back. She was clearly not over the jealousy thing yet.

Dad moved to the front of the group, stepped over the bodies, and shoved the door open. Conryu moved in front of Kelsie and brushed past his father. The rest of the group joined him just inside the door.

The demon stood and turned to face them. She rested her clawed hand on the mayor's neck in an unsubtle threat. Kelsie's hand felt warm on his back.

"I didn't expect to see you fools again. And you brought friends, how nice. The Society will give me a fine reward when I kill you, boy."

Conryu ignored her and focused. "By my will be bound, oh child of Hell. Your thoughts are my thoughts, your desires, my desires, Domination!"

Kelsie's power mingled with his as the spell surged out and settled over the succubus. It was stronger than the last time he used it and not just because of Kelsie's added power. It must have been the power boost the Dark Lady mentioned when they signed their agent contract.

The succubus snarled and twitched her head.

"Be still!" he commanded.

He focused the order on her body rather than her head as he had questions to ask before he sent her back. When her legs and arms went rigid he moved closer, his focus on the spell absolute.

"Release the mayor."

She growled and fought, the mayor staring straight ahead, seemingly unaware of anything happening around him.

Conryu took a step closer and locked gazes with her. "Do it!"

She screamed. A full-body shudder ran through the mayor and he slumped in his chair.

"Dad, Sarge, you guys want to pull him out of here?"

His father and Lin eased around the demon and slid the mayor's rolling office chair away from her before pushing him back behind the rest of the group.

"Where is the wizard in charge of the artifacts hiding?" Conryu pressed down on her with every bit of focus he could muster.

"I don't know."

With the spell on her the demon was incapable of lying. Her masters probably hadn't told her anything more than she needed to know for just this sort of eventuality. That meant she probably didn't have much in the way of useful information.

"You're the Dark Lady's new pet." The succubus sneered. "I can feel her presence running through your magic. She was never more than a second-rate whore. I don't know how she convinced you mortals that she's some sort of princess of demons."

"What is your name?"

The demon struggled but in the end his magic was stronger than her will. "Rennet."

"Rennet. I'll remember to mention you to the Dark Lady the next time we speak. I think you'll find her stronger now, a true princess. Terra, would you open the portal please?"

Behind him Terra chanted. "Reveal the way through infinite darkness. Open the path, Hell Portal!"

When the dark power from the open portal reached him Conryu said, "Back you go."

Rennet rose jerkily to her feet and shuffled over to the black disk. "You'll never find the last three boxes in time. This city will fall."

She jumped into the portal and Terra shut it behind her.

* * *

While Mr. and Mrs. Kane tried to bring the mayor back to the realm of the waking Conryu motioned his father off to one side. "How's Mom doing?"

The corner of his father's lip quirked up, about as strong a reaction as he ever gave. "You know your mother. She wasn't thrilled when I told her, but she's hanging in there. They have her working on a new project and it's helping her focus on something other than your problems."

"Do you think I should visit her now, or wait until this is over, one way or the other?"

"I don't know. If she sees you she'll get upset. That's just the way your mother is wired. But if things grow worse... I just don't know. Whatever you decide is fine with me."

"Thanks, Dad." Not that he'd been a great deal of help but it was nice just to talk about something other than magic and crazy wizards.

The mayor's groan drew Conryu's attention to the collection of people gathered around the semiconscious politician. Mrs. Kane was applying light magic healing in an effort to wake him faster while Maria looked on with a rapt expression. Whatever Maria's mom was doing, it appeared to be working.

Conryu took a step toward the group, but his father caught him by the arm. Conryu raised an eyebrow. "What's up?"

"I fought a demon today, son. For the first and god willing the last time. I wanted to tell you I have a whole new respect for the things you've done this year. Until I felt the creature's power with my own fists I didn't fully appreciate what fighting such a monster meant. I consider myself a strong warrior, but I couldn't even make it flinch."

Dad shook his head and Conryu wasn't certain what he should say. His father had never made such a long speech before, much less admitted any sort of weakness. The weirdness of it struck him dumb.

A few seconds later a louder groan from the mayor shook Conryu out of his stupor. "Don't worry, Dad. Dealing with things like demons is a job for wizards. Did you know the military considers us living weapons? Apparently that's all we are, weapons. Mr. Kane admitted the government regards us as assets more than individuals. I understand where they're coming from. Some of the things I can do now make me think they're right."

"No. You're not just a weapon, any more than I am. To an untrained person, what I can do is frightening, but it doesn't define me. We are more than the sum of our skills."

Conryu hugged his father. "Thanks, Dad. I think I will go see Mom before I go out again."

"What happened?" The mayor's mumbled question sounded like he was talking with a mouth full of marbles.

Conryu gave his father one last pat on the back and went over to join the others. The mayor was awake now and alternately staring and blinking at those around him. It didn't look like he was fully with it yet.

Mr. Kane crouched down in front of the mayor. "What's the last thing you remember, Tom?"

"Ugh." The mayor rubbed his eyes. "That woman. She said she came from Central to advise me on the current threat. She touched my shoulder. The next thing I know I'm looking at you lot."

"Loss of memory isn't uncommon in cases of psychic manipulation," Mrs. Kane said. "Demons are especially indifferent to any damage they may cause."

"Psychic manipulation? Demon? Maybe someone better tell me what's going on."

Conryu had heard enough. He slipped out the door to make the short run over to the science building. If the worst should happen he wanted to talk to his mother one last time.

Chapter 8

On the Run

Conryu jogged back to the Department building having spent a weepy ten minutes with his mother. Just as Dad had said, the moment she saw him Mom burst into tears and hugged him. When she finally brought herself under control Conryu gave her the sanitized version of his work so far. Even with the worst of the fights edited out she still almost started crying again.

Eventually, in desperation, he'd asked her about the project Dad mentioned. Changing the subject had worked wonders. She went on and on for ten minutes about how they were trying to fuse a nonmagical vehicle with a magical weapon, in this case a tank that shot fireballs. The military wanted to deploy it on the northern border to help deter the frost giants the next time they marched south.

He'd finally given her one last hug and made his escape. If he had any luck the others would have gotten the mayor up to speed and an order sent removing him from the city's most wanted list. The sun was hanging low in the sky and they didn't have a great deal of time left.

When he reached the conference room and opened the door everyone was seated at the long table. They all looked his way.

Maria stalked over. "Where have you been? We were trying to make plans, but without you we weren't sure of our next move."

"I went to see Mom. Anyway, what's to plan? Order the cops out of the way and I'll go smash those last three boxes and that'll be it."

"Just that easy?" She crossed her arms and stared.

"Simple, not easy, believe me. So are we good to go or what?"

Conryu looked over Maria's head. The mayor climbed to his feet, looking none too steady. "Come here, young man."

Maria took him by the hand and led him over to the mayor. He felt like a little kid being led to the principal's office. "Yes, sir?"

"Orin tells me I owe you my freedom as well as any hope that my city might survive the next day. I wanted to thank you and apologize for all the trouble you've been having with the police. I've spoken to all the station commanders. They'll have their people pulled back within the hour."

"That's a relief as we're getting low on time." He turned to Terra. "Just how long is left?"

She opened their laptop and clicked on something. "Eight hours."

"It's going to be close." Conryu scrubbed his hand across his face. "Jonny, Kelsie, let's get out of here. The cemetery isn't that far away."

"We'll be coming with you." Terra stood and was joined a moment later by Clair and Mrs. Kane.

"Me too." Maria moved to join the group, but her mother waved her back to the table.

"I know you want to help, sweetheart, but your magic isn't strong enough yet. Stay here with your father. We should have this wrapped up in an hour or two."

"Kelsie's weaker than I am and Jonny can't even use magic. How come they can go?"

"They can't." Terra glared at his friends. "We appreciate your help, but it's time to let the professionals handle this."

"You've done a bang-up job of it so far." Jonny crossed his arms and glared right back at the formidable wizard.

"I should go too." Kelsie sounded meeker, but no less determined. "If Conryu needs a power boost I can help."

"It's too dangerous," Terra said.

Jonny and Kelsie both looked at him like he had something to say about it. He sighed. "Kelsie did give me a boost when I dominated the succubus and Jonny's an excellent driver. I doubt I'd have gotten as far as I have without their help."

Part of him wanted to argue in Maria's favor too, but the bigger part would be happy knowing she was somewhere out of the immediate line of fire.

Terra's jaw clenched and relaxed as she grumbled under her breath. "Fine. We don't have time to argue anyway."

Maria hugged him and whispered, "Be careful."

He held her for a moment, soaking in the moment of peace. He doubted he'd have many more of them for the next little while. They broke apart and Maria hurried over to say goodbye to her mother.

Dad stepped closer, distracting him from the others. "You bring honor to the Koda Dojo and I am very proud of you, son."

They bowed to one another then Dad surprised him by taking him in a fierce embrace. "Come back safe."

The six of them left the Department building and headed to the parking lot. Conryu, Jonny, and Kelsie angled toward their stolen car. They hadn't gotten three steps when Terra said, "Where do you think you're going?"

"Our car?" Jonny raised an eyebrow.

"Speaking of cars." Mrs. Kane looked around the parking lot. "Where's mine?"

"It didn't explode," Conryu said. "But the cops shot it up pretty good. We had to abandon it in a parking garage. Jonny liberated that fine vehicle over there."

"You stole it?" Terra sounded horrified.

Conryu didn't blame her, but they hadn't had a ton of better options. "It was that or walk."

"Leave it there. It'd be a shame if you got arrested for driving a stolen car after we convinced the police to stop looking for you." Terra grimaced like she wanted to pull her hair out. His mom used to look like that all the time when he was a kid. "I'll ask Lin to deal with it later. We'll take Department cars. You three ride with Clair. I'll go with Shizuku."

* * *

Lady Raven paced in her casting chamber. She twisted her mask between her hands. On the scrying mirror the police were abandoning their posts protecting her artifacts. As soon as they moved out she switched the boxes back to their secondary hiding places, but that was only a temporary measure. Without the police present Conryu would make short work of locating the boxes and destroying the meager protections she'd put in place.

What the hell had happened to the council's agent? Everything was supposed to be under control on that end. If this was what passed for under control they were in big trouble.

Finally, the expected vibration ran through her mask. She tied it in place and rushed to the spell circle. The Hierarchs and Lady Bluejay were waiting.

"Our agent has been revealed and banished," Lady Dragon said without preamble.

"How?"

"The abomination dominated her and forced her to return to Hell," Lady Bluejay said. "Rennet contacted me as soon as she was able and alerted me to the situation."

"It's clear the leaders of the world have no intention of freeing our mistress or handing over the abomination." Lady Dragon's anger struck Lady Raven like a physical blow. "The artifacts must be activated at once, before any more of them are put out of commission."

"The island isn't yet in position," Lady Raven dared point out. If she activated them now all she could hope for was a handful of shadow beasts that would be instantly destroyed by any modestly powerful wizard that encountered them. They might kill fifteen or twenty people before they were hunted down, but not nearly enough to make a real impression.

"We are aware of that. With two artifacts already gone, there's no way we can complete the ritual as intended. Your new orders are to collect the remaining artifacts, carry them within range of the island, and activate them. I'll leave it up to your judgment where and how to accomplish your new task."

The connection was broken and Lady Raven was once more alone in her casting chamber. Things just kept getting worse. She tossed her mask onto the empty workbench and marched out of the chamber. At least it didn't appear that Lady Dragon held her personally responsible for the plan's failure. It was good fortune that another of the Society's agents had also come up short. That made her own failures less obvious.

Her guards fell in silently beside her as she made her way to the sewer access in the floor. She hardly even noticed the stink of rot surrounding the Faceless Ones' hosts anymore. That made Lady Raven wonder about her own smell, but only for a moment. If she succeeded in this final task it wouldn't matter if she smelled like a pigsty. The Hierarchs would be sure to forgive her earlier setbacks.

Outside the three rooms she'd prepared for her living quarters, the warehouse she'd chosen as her redoubt looked like you'd expect: filthy, run down, and filled with debris abandoned when the company that had owned it went out of business. The building was currently being argued over in court and neither the former owner nor his creditors had legal claim to it. That was one of the reasons she chose it as her base of operations: no one ever came to visit the place.

The other reason was built into the floor. At her mental command one of the Faceless Ones tossed aside a half-full crate revealing a steel manhole cover. The undead lifted the two-hundred-pound disk like it weighed nothing and set it aside.

In addition to their legitimate business operation the owners also ran a drug-smuggling business that used the hidden portal to come and go unseen. Lady Raven found it very useful for the exact same purpose.

She leapt down the concrete tube, whispering to the wind to slow her descent. A small platform rose above the muck and provided a relatively clean place for her to land. Beside it was a floating chariot big enough to hold her and her two guards. She'd made the thing over the winter, as much to alleviate her boredom as anything, but it had turned out to be a useful toy.

When she'd moved to one side two of her guards dropped down beside her, landing with bone-jarring force. The undead didn't even blink as they straightened up. The third remained behind at her mental command. If the worst happened she wanted at least one protector waiting for her return.

The three of them climbed aboard the chariot and with a thought Lady Raven activated the light spells carved into the front of the transport and sent it hurtling down the tunnel.

* * *

The little group reached the cemetery ten minutes later. The sun had set leaving them with nothing but twilight to work with. Conryu didn't know much about shadow beasts, but he knew enough to realize fighting them at night wasn't ideal since they were weaker in daylight.

Clair pulled the beat-up sedan off the road in front of a wrought iron gate leading into the cemetery grounds. He dearly wished she'd let Jonny drive. The woman was a menace behind the wheel. Conryu pulled his fingers free of the handle on the backseat door and flexed his stiff hand. She hadn't killed them all, but that was the only good thing about the trip.

There were no cops, but when Conryu checked there was no sign of the box either. The crypt that had once crackled with protective magic was now dark and empty. He scanned the rest of the cemetery, but found no magic of any sort.

"Are you seeing what I'm seeing?" Conryu wanted to be certain it wasn't just him missing something due to lack of experience.

"If you're seeing nothing but an empty cemetery then yes." Clair opened the door and they all piled out.

A few seconds later Terra and Mrs. Kane pulled up behind them and joined the group. They both stared out over the gravestones. "She moved it again," Terra said.

"Yeah." Conryu pushed the gate open and started up a low hill toward the crypt with Prime floating along beside him. "I'll have to track it through Hell."

Terra fell in beside him with the others bringing up the rear. "I'm interested to see how you follow the residual energy."

"I don't, I use Cerberus's nose." Conryu stopped in front of the crypt door. "There's nothing dangerous. She must have moved the box, protections and all."

"Yes, I suspect Mercia's been watching every move we make. When the police left the boxes probably did too." Terra's hands opened and closed as she talked.

"Mercia, huh? So I finally have a name for the woman that's caused me so much trouble." Conryu yanked the door open.

Mrs. Kane conjured light globes and sent them in. They revealed an empty chamber and three walls lined with rectangular doors labeled with the names of the bodies inside.

Conryu stepped inside, ignoring the musty, dust-filled air. "So who's going with me and who's following in the cars?"

Jonny immediately said, "Car."

Kelsie and Mrs. Kane agreed with him leaving Terra and Clair to join Conryu. When the others had retreated from the crypt Clair said, "I'll open the portal."

"No, I'd better do that. Cerberus will sense my magic and know it's me approaching. We really don't want to startle him.

Clair shrugged and didn't argue.

Conryu chanted, "Reveal the way through infinite darkness. Open the path. Hell Portal!"

The black disk appeared and he led the way through. Behind him Terra and Clair muttered unfamiliar spells then followed.

"Protective spells, Master," Prime said in answer to his unspoken question. "Neither of the wizards is dark aligned so traveling through Hell is as dangerous for them as it is for your friend."

Clair and Terra were both surrounded by glowing light magic auras. They looked around at the endless darkness, but neither appeared especially disconcerted.

A deep growl vibrated in his chest as Cerberus appeared beside him. Three pairs of eyes stared at Terra and Clair and he bared his fangs.

Conryu swatted his side. "Behave. These are friends."

"Cerberus doesn't care for their aura of light magic," Prime said. "That sort of energy is like a thorn in a demon's brain."

"Well then we need to do this as fast as possible. Cerberus, let's hunt."

All three heads barked and raised their noses in the air. It didn't take long for the demon dog to pick up the scent. A second bark preceded Cerberus crouching down to let Conryu climb up on his back. The moment he did Cerberus leapt into motion, racing through the darkness.

Conryu glanced back to make sure Terra and Clair were keeping up and relaxed when he saw they were. Before he knew it Cerberus skidded to a stop and barked a third time.

"Right here, huh? No demons at least." Whether that was a good thing or not Conryu couldn't say. He waited until the others were floating beside him. "Shall we take a look? Grant me the power to see through realms, Vision Gate!"

The window appeared, revealing a flying chariot racing down another sewer tunnel. "What the hell was that?" Of all the things he'd expected, a chariot soaring through the sewer was way down on the list.

"I didn't get a good look," Terra said. "But it had to be her."

"Why would she be fleeing the hiding place of one of her artifacts?" Clair scratched her head. "Shouldn't she want to defend it?"

"There's only one way to know for sure." Terra cast the portal spell.

They stepped into the damp stink of the sewer. Conryu was getting heartily sick of splashing around in shit rivers. When this was over he was never going underground again.

In front of them sat an empty pedestal. No wards guarded it and no shadow beasts roamed the area.

"She took the box with her." Terra slammed her fist into the slime-covered wall.

"What's she going to do, run around until the island is in place?" For the life of him Conryu couldn't figure out what Mercia's play was.

"She doesn't have to wait. Mercia can take the boxes to the island and activate the artifacts immediately." Terra dug her phone out. "Clair, make us a stone boat while I call Shizuku."

* * *

Lady Raven forced herself not to gloat, not even to herself. She'd beaten the Department wizards to the first box. She hadn't even seen any sign of them. The fools were so far behind they wouldn't know what happened until her shadow beasts ripped the life from them.

The chariot raced down the tunnels as smooth and silent as the wind. In the darkness beside her the shadow tigers effortlessly kept pace. It had been only a moment's work to alter the binding that compelled them to guard the box into one that made them protect her. She doubted the creatures would last long in a fight, but having them might be the difference between success and failure.

Up ahead the sewer split left and right. A mental command turned her transport down the right-hand branch. Another advantage she held was Lady Raven already knew where the boxes were hidden while her hunters had to track them down individually. She smiled as she pictured the frustrated grimace on Terra's face. It would have been nice to be there in person, but that would most assuredly not prove wise.

The next pedestal waited many miles away. Now that she had to collect the artifacts Lady Raven found herself wishing she hadn't hidden them so far apart. Of course, that had been less a personal choice and more a necessity of the ritual she'd planned. If everything had gone according to that plan, she would have opened the largest dark portal in history. For the crime of denying her that honor she'd rip Conryu Koda's heart out and feed it to her pets.

A pair of the shadow tigers surged ahead and a moment later a man in a hardhat and coveralls appeared in the chariot lights. A second later he went down under the insubstantial claws of her guardians. She rushed by the corpse and the two tigers fell back in place. The worker hadn't been a threat, but she didn't chastise the creatures. Giving them a snack now and then made the beasts easier to control.

She continued on for a couple more minutes, nothing and no one disturbing the darkness ahead of her. A mile from the next hiding place she sensed something approaching from behind. She darted a glance over her shoulder. Way behind her a dot of light glimmered in the dark. It was too far away to make out anything, but instinct said it had to be her enemies.

They must have stumbled on her trail at the first pedestal. Lady Raven grinned. She was far enough ahead to collect the next box and leave a nasty surprise for the fools trailing her.

* * *

The tunnel walls blurred as the stone boat raced through the sewers. Conryu had never seen a stone boat much less ridden in one before today. The thing looked like exactly what the name implied, a canoe made of stone that hovered six inches above the tunnel floor.

Clair tried to explain how she charged the stone of the floor with a different frequency of magic than the one she used on the boat and that the two powers pushed against each other causing it to levitate, but his eyes just glazed over. It worked and that was enough for him.

Since she was directing the boat Clair sat in the front with Terra behind her and Conryu in the rearmost seat. The back of Terra's head and her streaming hair obscured his vision. He caught an occasional glimpse of the wall as they whipped by, but otherwise he was blind. Terra muttered constantly as she tracked the energy of Mercia's chariot. Conryu wanted to help, but such finely tuned magic was still beyond him. If they needed something smashed he was ready to step up.

"I see a light," Clair said.

Conryu moved left then right, trying to look around Terra. He caught a glimpse of something—he thought he did anyway, it might have been his imagination.

"It's her." Terra had stopped her muttering. Maybe now that they were closer she didn't need the spell to help her track Mercia. "Step on it."

"I'm giving it all I can. It's not like there's a gas pedal."

"Conryu, switch places with me."

Conryu and Terra shifted and shimmied around each other, causing the boat to wobble and drawing a barely audible curse from Clair.

When they finally swapped positions Terra put her back against his. "Hang on. Father of winds grant this unworthy servant of fire the loan of your breath, Gust!"

Terra slammed into his back and the boat rushed forward at almost double the speed. The light ahead quickly grew brighter.

"Too much, Terra!" Clair had to shout over the roar of the wind. "I can't control the boat. Your wind magic is destabilizing my earth spell."

The shadows ahead shifted. Conryu had seen that before. "We've got company coming."

He'd barely gotten the warning out when a shadowy tiger lunged into the light of the flames. With both women fully occupied it fell to him to protect everyone.

Conryu thrust his hand toward the lunging beast. "All things burn to ash, Inferno Blast!"

The flames incinerated the tiger in a second.

"There are more, Master," Prime said from where he huddled under the lip of the boat.

Conryu's gaze darted left and right, trying to pick out the beasts' movements from the flickering shadows. He shot another burst of flame, but hit only stone.

Clair screamed and the boat spun out of control. They slammed into the right wall, bounced off, and crashed into the left side. Conryu's brain rattled in his head. He caught a glimpse of a dark claw withdrawing from the front of the boat.

"Are you okay?" Conryu didn't dare look at her.

"Yeah, my light barrier held, but that still hurt like a son of a bitch."

Behind him Terra had ended her spell. She hissed and the light grew brighter. Circling them at the edge of the shadows were five more tigers.

He scrambled to his feet and hurled a stream of fire at one, but the beast easily dodged. "Any suggestions, ladies?"

"I can deal with the tigers if you can keep them at bay for a minute," Terra said.

"I'll do my best."

Terra didn't reply as she'd already fallen into the rhythm of her spell. Conryu threw both hands forward and waved the flames around, simulating a wall of flames. Behind him the power of Terra's spell grew.

Clair stayed huddled in the stone boat with Prime, rubbing her temples, and giving her head an occasional shake. Looked like she'd gotten the worst of it in the crash.

"Duck!" Terra shouted.

Conryu clenched his fists and dropped back into the boat. A rush of flame that filled the tunnel from ceiling to floor streaked down the monsters. After its passing the stone gleamed and there was no sign of the shadow beasts.

"You destroyed them all," Prime confirmed. "However I sense more up ahead, their presence is faint but I believe it's another six beasts."

Conryu looked up at a sweating, limp Terra. That spell must have taken a lot out of her. He turned to Clair. "I think we'll have to handle the next bunch."

"Earth magic is useless against insubstantial enemies and my fire and light skills aren't what I'd like them to be."

"You can help a little though, right?" If he had to rely on the simple fire spell Sonja had taught him they might be in trouble.

"I'll do all I can. Climb aboard, Terra. The boat's ready to go."

They took their seats. Conryu remained in the middle in case he needed to blast anything while Terra slumped in the rear, eyes closed and panting for breath.

Clair guided them down the tunnel at a more cautious pace. No one wanted to fly straight into another ambush. The only thing that reassured him was the knowledge that Prime would warn him if the shadow beasts attacked.

A few minutes later, after who knew how many hundreds of yards, they spotted another light ahead of them. It didn't seem like they'd gone fast enough to catch up to Mercia, so who knew what type of trap she'd left this time.

"Reveal." The light was magical, but his spell revealed nothing else. He squinted, trying to make out what was glowing. "It's not moving."

"It's not Mercia." Terra shifted behind him. Her voice sounded strong; he took that as a good sign. "She's further away."

"As are the shadow beasts," Prime added.

"Want me to dispel it?" The closer they inched to the light the itchier he felt. It had to be a trap. Of course it might be a trap that went off when he tried to dispel it, like last winter with the demons.

"No. Clair, stop well back from it and we'll approach on foot. I don't want to blunder into anything."

"Every minute we waste, Mercia's lead grows." Conryu couldn't see Clair's expression, but the frustration in her voice came through loud and clear. He understood that. Sometimes it seemed like every step they made was in the wrong direction.

"We won't stop her if we're all blown up."

Clair grumbled, but eased the boat along until the head-sized sphere of light came into view. Conryu frowned. Why would a dark wizard like Mercia set a trap using light magic? It didn't make sense.

"Okay, Conryu," Terra said.

He crossed his fingers and wrists. "Darkness dispels everything."

The orb of dark magic struck the sphere and it vanished in an instant. The moment it did a magical vibration ran through him. A wall of flames sprang to life and came rushing at them.

Conryu raised his arms and hoped he lived through the next five seconds.

* * *

Jonny drove along at twenty miles an hour, following Maria's mom's directions. He hated the Department car. The steering was loose, the suspension sucked, and every pothole sent a spring up his ass. Surely they had better cars than this for their employees. It wasn't even an improvement over the piece of shit he hot-wired in the garage, leaving aside the fact that it wasn't stolen.

He sighed. Cars he understood, the whole magic thing, not so much. Apparently Mrs. Kane was following Conryu and the others' path through the sewers. He glanced in the rearview mirror. Kelsie had her nose pressed to the window as if she could somehow peer through the pavement down to the tunnels. The girl had a serious crush on his clueless best friend.

Whatever trick Mrs. Kane was using, it wasn't one Kelsie knew. Not surprising given she was only a freshman. Then again, Conryu was a freshman and he could open portals to Hell, had a pet giant three-headed demon hound, and whatever spell he'd used in the parking garage that gave Jonny chills just thinking about it. The noises the cops had made when those black spirits passed through them would haunt his dreams for the rest of his life.

Jonny thought of Conryu like a brother, but damn. The shit he could do wasn't right.

"Turn left," Mrs. Kane said.

He frowned. There wasn't a street to turn down. A little later they reached an intersection and he made the left. Hopefully it wouldn't screw up her spell.

Two blocks later she said, "Stop."

He parked under a light across the street from a pizzeria. His mouth started watering. The army was good about getting them their three squares a day, but the food left a great deal to be desired.

Mrs. Kane left the car and Jonny and Kelsie joined her.

"Did they stop?" Kelsie hurried around the car and stood beside Mrs. Kane. "Are they fighting?"

"They did stop, but I don't sense any fighting. It's possible they lost her trail. Do either of you see any manhole covers?"

Jonny scanned up the street. There was usually one every few hundred yards. Of course it could be in the shadows between street lights.

The ground shook and something exploded. He spun just as one of the thick steel disks went flying into the air about fifty feet before crashing into the street.

"There's one."

The ladies ignored his attempt at humor and ran for the opening. Kelsie reached it first and started for the ladder hammered into the side of the shaft.

Mrs. Kane grabbed her collar. "Let me check and make sure we're not dropping down into a trap or the middle of a battle."

She muttered something in one of those weird languages the wizards spoke and nodded. "It's clear."

Before she could resume her descent Conryu's face appeared at the bottom of the shaft.

"You okay, bro?"

"Yeah, but Clair's pretty banged up. She took the brunt of the blast. I can't climb up with her and Terra's too exhausted to cast."

"Move her into position, Conryu," Mrs. Kane said. "I'll use a wind spell to lift her up."

Conryu didn't immediately move. "She's earth aligned. Will wind magic be okay?"

"For the three seconds I'll need to lift her it'll be fine. Hurry now."

He nodded and disappeared back into the darkness. A minute later he returned carrying Clair in his arms. He stood her up against the ladder and held her in place while Mrs. Kane cast another spell.

Wind swirled and carried the unconscious woman up along with the stench of the sewer. Jonny's appetite died in an instant. When Clair had flown all the way out of the opening Jonny caught her and carried her to the car. Kelsie ran over and opened the back door. He laid her on the seat and wiped the sweat from his brow.

Mrs. Kane nodded to Jonny. "Help Conryu. Terra's in no shape to climb on her own."

"Got it." He jogged back to the opening, ignoring the people that had gathered to stare, and looked down. A moment later Conryu appeared with Terra's arm around his shoulders. The wizard's head lolled around like her neck had turned to rubber and her eyes fluttered, half open, half closed. "What can I do?"

"Reach down and grab the back of her robe. I'll push from this end."

Terra muttered something, but it was nonsense to Jonny. Real nonsense, not the magical nonsense he'd gotten used to over the last day. Between them he and Conryu pulled and shoved the incoherent wizard out of the sewer. It was an absolute miracle no cars came along while they were in the middle of the road.

"I have her," Conryu said when she was out. His creepy book flew up beside him a moment later. "Can you slide the cover into place? We don't want someone busting an axle in the hole."

"No problem."

Jonny dragged the cover back where it belonged and joined the others beside the car. In the back seat Clair was encased in a glowing box of white energy. It was just transparent enough to allow him to watch her bruises and scrapes fading away.

Conryu had Terra in the passenger seat and Mrs. Kane held a glowing hand over the woozy wizard's heart. When the light faded Terra's eyes were closed and she started snoring.

Mrs. Kane turned to Conryu. "What happened?"

Conryu sat on the hood and rubbed the bridge of his nose. Though he looked tired, he was in way better shape than the other two. Jonny wished there was something he could do to help, but when it came to magic he was just a bystander.

"We ran into a trap. There was a sphere of light magic which drew our attention, but it was a decoy. When I dispelled it another spell activated which caused the blast. I thought we were going to get roasted alive, but I summoned a dark magic barrier, by instinct more than anything and it negated the worst of the blast. Terra turned aside some of the heat I missed, but Clair was struck by flying debris."

"We were stupid." Terra's eyes had opened after her brief nap. "I assumed since Mercia is a dark-aligned wizard she'd set a dark magic trap and that's what I searched for. I never imagined she'd combine light and fire magic. My overconfidence almost got us killed."

"Clair and I didn't think of it either." Trust Conryu to try and shoulder his share of the blame. He couldn't help himself. For as long as Jonny had known him Conryu had believed he was responsible whenever anything happened, even if there was nothing he could have done to stop it.

"You're a freshman, barely into your training, and Clair doesn't have the experience I do. I've been a government wizard for twenty-seven years and I walked into that trap like a first-year rookie. We're going to have to do a lot better if we want to survive and stop Mercia."

Jonny was suddenly glad, for the first time today, to be a bystander. If it had fallen to him to figure this mess out he didn't know how he'd handle it.

Chapter 9

Hide and Seek

Conryu paced and tried to ignore the faces pressed up against the glass of the pizzeria window across the street. Clair had been under the effect of the healing spell for fifteen minutes and the worst of her visible injuries had disappeared. Mrs. Kane was pouring energy into Terra to counteract the backlash that had turned her brain to mush.

He glanced at Kelsie who was watching every move he made as if she feared he might collapse at any moment. He wasn't in that bad a shape, but it had been a long day and it showed no sign of ending soon. There was still one box to go, the one from the culvert. At the rate she was flying he figured Mercia should be there soon if she hadn't arrived already.

There was no way to stop her from collecting the last one. What they needed now was to figure out how to keep her from activating them. Unfortunately, Conryu hadn't a clue how to go about it. Assuming Terra was right and Mercia was planning to go directly to the island's shadow and activate the artifacts they didn't have much time.

Conryu patted his pockets. Where was that stupid phone? "Hey, Jonny, do you have the phone? I need to talk to Lin."

Jonny dug the little flip phone out of his pocket and tossed it over. Conryu autodialed and a moment later Maria picked up. "Are you okay? Is everything alright?"

"I'm fine, but we've run into a roadblock. Is Lin there? I need to talk to him."

There was a clunk and a pair of taps then Lin said, "Conryu? What do you need?"

"Do you have the map with the island's path on it handy?"

"Just a second." Silence was followed by the faint clattering of keys. "Okay, go ahead."

"Draw a circle one mile in diameter around the culvert location. When you have that overlay all sewer exits. Assuming she can't activate the artifacts underground she'll have to come out of one of them."

More tapping was followed by, "I have three potential exit points between the culvert and the island. Seven if you branch out further."

"Awesome, thanks, Sarge. Can you email all seven to Terra's phone?"

Jonny approached as he hung up. "We got a plan?"

"That might be generous. How are the patients?"

"Still breathing, though I think Terra fell back asleep. So what now?"

"Now we find a high place where we can see most of the exits Sarge found and hope she doesn't come flying out before we arrive."

* * *

Lady Raven couldn't stop smiling as she collected the final box. When those fools had blundered into her trap the heat from the explosion had singed her back and warmed her heart. With a fire wizard and a dark wizard amongst them it was unlikely she'd managed to kill anyone, but she'd gotten them off her trail and that was all she really needed. A smoldering pile of corpses would have been a nice bonus though.

She climbed back onto the chariot between her two guardians. The section of sewer where she'd hidden the final box didn't connect to the section under the island and she needed to be above ground to trigger the artifacts anyway. With just a little luck she might be able to form a proper magical triad and still open a decent-sized portal. It wouldn't be as impressive as what she originally planned, but it would get the Society's point across.

With a mental command she sent the chariot hurtling down the tunnel. It was a short flight to the nearest access and a few seconds later she stopped again. Directly ahead was a grate that led to a processing plant. She hardly thought it possible, but the stench from the plant was worse than the sewers themselves. When her mission was complete Lady Raven planned to take a week-long bath with scented water.

She chanted, "Rust and rot, all things become nothing, Entropic Wave!"

A wave of her hand sent dark energy toward the grate. When the energy had passed by, all that remained were flecks of rust. The chariot shot through the opening, flying over tanks of filthy water, and smashing through a skylight and into the clean, fresh air.

Lady Raven took a deep breath of the cool night air. If she never had to go in another sewer it would be a fine thing. She turned the chariot towards the island. It wasn't much beyond a mile to the outer edge of the shadow. As soon as she reached it she'd land and finish her task.

* * *

They were three blocks down the road when Terra woke up again. Conryu was smushed in the back seat between Kelsie and Mrs. Kane—not the worst pair to get sandwiched between now that he thought about it—while Clair remained in the healing field. He didn't know for sure, but it seemed like she must have had some internal injuries from the blast if she wasn't out of it yet.

Prime rested on his lap. The scholomantic had stayed uncharacteristically quiet since the explosion. Given their connection, Conryu assumed he'd know if Prime sustained any serious damage. Not that there was anything he could do about it. Light magic healing didn't work on demons.

Jonny had Terra's phone open on the dash in front of him, the map Lin had sent pulled up on the screen. A quick search had turned up a twelve-story apartment building with a rooftop garden situated within sight of five of the potential exits. While it didn't offer complete coverage it was the best option available.

"Where are we going?" Terra yawned and rubbed her eyes.

Conryu gave her the gist of his very sketchy plan. When he finished she looked back at him. "I'm impressed. Your plan shows initiative and quick thinking. It's far from perfect, but given our circumstances I can't come up with anything better."

"Thanks, I guess."

Terra's gaze shifted to Clair. "How is she?"

"I don't believe she's in any danger." Mrs. Kane made a mystic pass over the field. "The magic will end when all her injuries are fully healed. It takes as long as it takes."

"That's about what I figured." Terra turned back around.

Fifteen minutes later they parked in front of the apartment building. Lights shone from most of the windows and a low buzz of music filled the air. Just normal people on an ordinary weekday night. Conryu envied them their ignorance, for a moment anyway.

He'd come to realize over the past year that with ignorance came helplessness. Should a shadow beast show up he doubted anyone in the building would be able to do anything but scream and die. It was up to him and the others to make sure that didn't happen. It was a heavy responsibility and one that set his stomach churning whenever he thought too hard about it.

Terra, Jonny, Kelsie, and Conryu started toward the building, leaving Mrs. Kane with the still-healing Clair. It was a short walk to the front door.

As they walked Conryu asked, "Can I control the path of the Dispel spheres I throw or do they only go in a straight line?"

"As always, Master, your will controls your magic. Simply focus on the path you wish the spell to take and it will oblige. The only reason you shot them straight up to now is that it never occurred to you there was any other option."

"Are you okay? You've been quieter than usual today."

"Too many people, Master. Demons like me are solitary, seeking new knowledge on our own. Being around so many others is uncomfortable so I entered a state of reduced awareness."

"From now on I'm going to need you on your game, so no napping. Right?"

"Yes, Master."

They reached the doors and Terra pushed through. Inside was a lobby with a fat, middle-aged man sitting behind a desk sipping coffee. He looked up when they entered, his eyes bugging out when his gaze settled on Prime.

"You lot aren't residents, so you visiting someone?" His gaze darted to and from Prime, as though he feared the book might bite his face off.

"We require access to your rooftop garden," Terra said in that official tone that added a silent or else.

The security man seemed to hear it, but he still said, "It's against the rules for anyone but building residents to go up there."

Terra leaned in so their noses were almost touching. "I'm with the Department of Magic and this is a citywide security emergency. Pursuant to City Code Twenty-Three A, all city officials shall have access to any nonresidential space necessary to complete their duties. Anyone obstructing said activities will face a fine of not less than twenty thousand dollars or five years in prison."

"Okay, okay." He dug through the drawer in his desk and came up with a key. "Here. This unlocks the roof door."

Terra snatched it out of his hand and marched towards a nearby bank of elevators. When everyone had gotten onboard and the doors closed Conryu said, "I'm impressed you had that law memorized. I've never even heard of it."

"Of course you haven't. I made it up just now. I've discovered over the years that quoting a law, even one that doesn't exist, will generally convince civilians to do what you want."

Conryu grinned. He didn't think the uptight wizard had a sneaky bone in her body.

"What happens if he looks it up?" Jonny asked.

"Who cares? We'll be on the roof already. Besides, have you ever tried to look something up on the government website? This will be settled before he can figure out for sure I was lying."

"He didn't strike me as the type to go out of his way," Kelsie said. "I bet he just closes his eyes and tries to pretend we were a dream."

The elevator chimed and the door opened revealing a hall that ended in a door labeled "roof access." A pair of big sodium lights illuminated a rooftop garden consisting of a mixture of vegetables, flowers, and lawn. There was a picnic table with an umbrella where people could have lunch.

Floating over the city, the island was a dark area blocking the stars. That's where Mercia was headed. Conryu tried to orient himself. Which way would she be coming from? He turned left. That way, he was pretty sure.

"I need to teach you a spell," Terra said. "It's a simple water spell that will enhance your vision so you can better aim at Mercia."

Terra spoke three words that sounded sort of gurgly, like she was trying to talk with a mouth full of water, and made a pass across her eyes with her left hand.

Conryu mimicked her. His eyes tingled and when he looked at the sprawling city it was like looking through powerful binoculars. "Neat trick."

"The spell warps the water particles in the air, creating a magnification effect. Simple, but very useful in this line of work. Everyone pick a corner and keep your eyes open. If you see anything flying give a shout."

They had barely gotten in position when Kelsie shouted, "I see something!"

Conryu ran over to her and squinted in the direction she was pointing. In response to his desire the spell zoomed in. There she was. Mercia and her two zombies riding in that flying chariot. "Are you up to giving me a boost?"

Kelsie beamed, ducked around behind him, and put her hand on his back. Conryu raised his own arm and focused his will on Mercia, or more precisely, the chariot. "Break!"

The globe of dark energy streaked out, guided by his will, tracking her like a heat-seeking missile.

* * *

Lady Raven sensed a tingle from a spell an instant before it struck. The chariot disintegrated under her and she was falling.

She tossed the boxes away and began the swirling gestures of a wind spell. The pavement was approaching rapidly when the spell kicked in and slowed her descent. Her feet slammed into the ground, sending pain running up her calves and into her thighs.

A short ways away her guardians picked themselves up off the pavement looking none the worse for the fall. Short of powerful magic the undead were nearly indestructible. She took a limping step and winced. Pity she couldn't say the same thing about herself.

"Hey, are you alright?" A young man and his girlfriend came running towards her.

She didn't know if they witnessed her fall from the sky, but her limp was pretty hard to miss. The pair paused a short ways away, frowning with concern.

She took another step and stumbled. The man reached out to steady her. The moment he made contact she said, "Your soul is mine, Lifetaker!"

He shriveled up to nothing and the woman screamed.

Lady Raven winced. She needed to draw more attention like she needed a hole in the head. She gave the nearest undead a mental command and it caved the woman's head in with a single blow from its massive fist.

Lady Raven straightened and took a pain-free step. Much better. Now to collect the boxes. The necroplasma coating would have protected them from any damage, the trick would be discovering where they'd landed. They shouldn't be too far away at least.

She had to hurry. Only one person was strong enough to cast a Dispel that powerful. It seemed her hunters had recovered and were once more on her trail.

* * *

Conryu and the others rushed back to the elevator. The security guard looked up at their approach, but they just waved, tossed him back his key, and kept going. When his Dispel blast had twisted and followed Mercia's chariot just like he wanted it to Conryu had been so excited he almost lost his focus.

Terra hadn't allowed them a moment to celebrate, insisting the fall would at most inconvenience their prey and slow her down a little. They made a rough note of where she should've landed and ran for the elevator.

Outside, Clair and Mrs. Kane were leaning against the car. Clair still looked pale, but she no longer had any visible injuries. Hopefully her magic was restored as well. They'd need everyone to hunt down the elusive Mercia.

"Get in!" Terra shouted. "She's down, but not out."

Jonny leapt behind the wheel and started the engine. This time Conryu got stuck between Clair and Kelsie. Also not terrible if you overlooked Clair's scowl.

Tires squealed as Jonny pulled away from the curb and accelerated down the street. Conryu estimated they were two miles from where Mercia went down, but that was as the crow flies. Taking the streets it might be double that.

Conryu glanced at Clair. "You okay?"

"Yeah. Shizuku said you carried me out, thanks."

"She's being modest. I only carried you as far as the ladder. Mrs. Kane lifted you out with wind magic then Jonny carried you to the car for healing. It was a total group effort."

"You're supposed to say 'you're welcome' and shut up."

"Oh, you're welcome." He shut up which brought a giggle from Kelsie. He turned her way. "Thanks for the power boost up there. Was it me or did it feel stronger than during the finals?"

"I thought so too, but I feared I was imagining things so I didn't want to say anything."

"You're getting closer to your full potential. That can only be a good thing."

Jonny took a hard corner, throwing them together and making him wish they had four seat belts in the back instead of just three.

"And she says I drive too fast," Clair muttered around a faint smile.

"Slow down, we're getting close." Terra had donned a pair of wire-rimmed glasses that would have looked right at home in a picture from a hundred years ago.

Jonny eased off the gas. A horrible shriek of crushed steel grated in Conryu's ears a moment before the car went tumbling sideways.

Metal crunched and he just managed to grab a hold of Kelsie's shoulder strap. Conryu braced himself enough to keep from bashing his head in. The car rolled twice before settling on its crumpled roof.

Upside down and dazed, Conryu tried to figure out what just hit them. A dull roar was followed by the opposite side door being ripped off its hinges. A big man with black eyes and a slack expression appeared in the opening.

Conryu thrust his hand at it. "All things burn to ash, Inferno Blast!"

The flames shot past Mrs. Kane and struck the undead monster square in the chest, forcing it back. They used the momentary respite to pile out of the car on the side farthest from the creature.

Conryu peeked over the wreck. His blast had burned the shirt off the ugly thing and nothing more. The undead grabbed the car, crumpling the steel with its bare hands, and pushed it toward them.

Clair laid a finger on the car and spoke a short phrase. The car stopped and despite its moaning efforts the monster couldn't budge it.

Terra took advantage of the distraction to point her still glove-covered hand at the undead and chant. A fist made of flame as tall as Conryu hammered the monster and sent it flying back across the street. It crashed into the side of an apartment building, taking a chunk out of the concrete.

A skinny bald man stepped out onto the stoop. "What's going on out here? People are trying to sleep."

The undead ripped a chunk of cement the size of Conryu's head out of the side of the building and drew back like it planned to throw it. Conryu pointed. "Shatter!"

The stone collapsed to dust.

"Get back inside!" Jonny waved his hands as though shooing an animal the direction he wanted it to go.

The man didn't need any more encouraging. He rushed back in, slamming the door behind him. With any luck he'd warn the other tenants and keep them out of harm's way.

The undead tried to climb back to its feet, but Terra's flaming fist smashed down on it again. It didn't look like it was doing much damage, but at least the thing wasn't trying to rip them apart. The undead struggled yet again to rise and yet again the fist came crashing down, this time smashing a piece out of the side of the building on its way down.

"This isn't going to work," Conryu said. "If you keep it up you'll bring the building down."

"I doubt even that would stop it." Clair had ended whatever spell she'd used to keep the car from moving.

"Yeah, I imagine the people living inside wouldn't appreciate it either." Conryu moved around in front of the car. "Let it up for a second. Cloak of Darkness."

As the protective magic settled over him, Terra's flaming fist went up into the sky. This time the undead clambered to its feet without interference.

Conryu pointed at its head. "Shatter!"

Flesh and blood disintegrated, leaving only the bare skull. That got its attention. The monster charged, its heavy tread cracking the pavement with each stride.

When it was in the middle of the street Conryu said, "Now!"

The fist came crashing down. The undead dodged at the last second and kept coming. A fist like a Christmas ham came for Conryu's head far faster than it had any right to. He dodged left and struck the passing forearm with a double palm thrust. His bare-fisted blow didn't do any damage, but the force of the impact launched him clear of the undead and gave him breathing room.

Instead of punching, Terra's fist opened and wrapped around the undead's torso, pinning its arms to its sides. A lightning bolt lanced in, staggering the monster a step. The pavement at its feet turned into a pair of hands that grasped its ankles.

They had it immobilized, but that wouldn't last. As if to prove it the monster shrugged massive shoulders and ripped the flaming fist apart. It punched the first stone hand to gravel and reared back for the second one.

"Reveal the way through infinite darkness. Open the path, Hell Portal!" Conryu opened a gate directly under the undead's feet. At the same moment Clair released it from the remaining stone hand, sending the monster tumbling out of sight.

"Mercia can just call it back to her with a portal of her own," Terra said. "We'll end up fighting it a second time."

"Cerberus! Tear it apart!" Conryu let the portal close. "If she can make any use of the scraps of flesh left over when Cerberus finishes, she's a better wizard than I thought."

Terra didn't comment, instead turning her gaze up the street. "The boxes are on the move. This way."

With no other options, they jogged after her.

* * *

Lady Raven felt the Faceless One she'd sent to ambush Terra and her companions vanish. She'd hoped the powerful undead would have lasted longer, at least long enough for her to reach the shadow. Regardless, it had done enough. She had a sufficient lead that there was no way for her pursuers to catch her before she activated the first artifact.

She ducked down a garbage-strewn alley and glanced up at the island. The base of the island was so dark she could make it out more by the absence of stars than anything. Light from the apartments above filtered down into the alley. It wasn't much, but the meager glow allowed her to save her magic and at this point every speck of power she could hold back was precious.

Only a few hundred more yards. Her last guardian thumped along beside her, the three boxes tucked under its massive arm, as impassive as a moving statue. That was the best thing about working with undead. They didn't care if one of their comrades was destroyed. In fact she wasn't even sure if the dim-witted creature was aware of its fellow's demise.

At the end of the alley she paused, trying to figure out the best location for the first point of the triangle. The wall beside her exploded, showering her with stones.

"Mercia!" Terra and her group stood at the far end of the alley. The bitch was wearing the gauntlet Lady Raven had provided for Iron Skull when the biker still lived. It would have been a delightful irony if she wasn't the one getting hit with it. "Surrender now and I'll do my best to make sure you aren't executed."

"Ha. That'll be the day." Lady Raven pointed and wiggled her fingers. "Threads from the deepest pit bind my enemies and crush them to nothing, Black Tentacles!"

Dozens of black, amorphous threads like worms a foot in diameter rushed down the alley. Halfway to Terra a monstrous burst of dark magic consumed them all. When the midnight energy cleared the abomination appeared, standing beside Terra.

He was too strong for her to fight head on and anyway she only needed two or three more minutes. She turned to her guardian. "Give me those and stop them."

She took the boxes and ran, leaving her final protector to buy her time.

* * *

"Why'd you give her a chance to surrender?" Conryu asked Terra as Mercia disappeared around the end of the alley. He wasn't a bloodthirsty person, but with everything on the line even Conryu recognized Mercia had to be stopped regardless of what it took.

The undead thing turned to face them and charged. He was really getting to hate those monsters. Lucky for him this was the last one she had with her.

"Reveal the way through infinite darkness. Open the path, Hell Portal!" The disk opened in front of the monster, but it leapt over the portal and kept coming.

That was new. The ugly thing hadn't even seen him cast that spell before. He closed the portal and Terra sent a flaming fist roaring at the monster. The undead brought its hands together and smashed the magic aside like it was nothing.

Ten feet from them hands of stone sprang up and grasped its ankles. It hit the ground hard, sending vibrations through the soles of Conryu's boots. A second later golden chains wrapped around the monster, holding it down.

"Go after her!" Clair said. "We'll deal with this one."

Conryu shared a look with Terra, who nodded. They ran down the alley and hooked a left. Mercia couldn't have gotten that far ahead of them.

Outside the alley the street was pitch black. No light shone from the streetlights and the island blotted out the moon and stars. Jonny and Kelsie pounded up behind them.

"Which way?" Conryu asked.

Terra peered left and right through her old-fashioned glasses.

"Can you even see anything?" Conryu could barely make out Jonny's silhouette against the light from the alley.

"Don't distract her," Kelsie said. "She's searching for magical energy, not footprints. No extra light needed."

A crash sounded from behind them. He hoped Clair and Mrs. Kane could handle the undead on their own.

A pair of flame globes sprang into being. Conryu squinted against the sudden glare.

"She went right." At Terra's gesture the globes drifted off down the street.

They ran after the globes, Conryu straining to hear anything that might be an attack, but the area was silent.

They hadn't gone far when the already cool night grew even colder.

"No!" Terra picked up her pace.

A hundred yards up the street was a small park, not much more than a patch of grass with a small fountain and a pair of benches. A figure in black stood beside the fountain, on its lip rested a dark, rectangular object that radiated dark magic so strong he could sense it without using the detection spell.

Terra threw her hand forward. "Flames of destruction incinerate my enemy, Fire Blast!"

A line of flames streaked toward Mercia, but struck a dark magic barrier a foot short of their target. "Mercia! Don't!"

There was just enough light to allow Conryu to catch her smile as she opened the lid.

Chapter 10

The Portal Opens

Maria tapped her toe and stared out the huge window in her father's office. It was almost midnight, but thousands of windows, headlights and streetlights lit the city below. The tiny dots of brightness soothed her and filled her with hope, like each one represented a life out in the emptiness of the night.

Conryu's parents sat together in the guest chairs. Sho had his arm around his wife and while his face remained impassive the tightness at the corners of his eyes betrayed his worry. Conryu's mom, on the other hand, was a bundle of nerves, alternating between rocking back and forth, kneading her head, and rubbing her bloodshot eyes.

Maria knew how they felt. Waiting and worrying about Conryu had gotten to be her new hobby. The mayor had appropriated her father's desk and was shouting into the phone with no more success than he'd enjoyed for the past hour. It looked like the city really was on its own.

"Why don't you take a break, Tom?" Dad guided the mayor to one of the spare chairs they'd dragged in to accommodate all the extra people.

"How can they refuse to send anyone?" The mayor sounded baffled. "We're facing one of the gravest crises in the city's history. If Central can't help us now, what good are they?"

Her father clearly didn't have any answers for the mayor. Maria blinked. Maybe she did. "What about calling in the academy teachers for backup? Everyone's on break so they should be free."

Dad rushed over to his desk and grabbed the phone. "That's a great idea, sweetheart. I don't know if any of them are still at the school, but it's worth a shot."

Maria clutched her chest as a shooting pain ran through her. Someone had just unleashed powerful dark magic. She looked back out the window and her eyes widened as a black pillar shot up into the sky. It struck the bottom of the island and immediately tripled in diameter.

"Tell them to hurry. We don't have much time."

Dad looked up from the phone. He dropped the receiver and reached for her. "What's wrong?"

Maria nodded toward the window.

Her father turned and gasped. "What is that?"

"I don't know the name for it, but Conryu was trapped in one during the Awakening ceremony. I think it's a sort of dark portal."

"Mercia must have activated one of the artifacts. Lin!"

"Sir?"

She'd forgotten all about the laconic detective leaning against the wall off by himself. He pushed off and ambled over to the desk.

"Did you take those enchanted guns out to the police stations?"

"Sure, but with everyone focused on Conryu I doubt they were ever deployed."

"Well get out there, round them up, and head to the portal. The wizards are going to need backup. I'll have the civilian casters I contacted earlier meet you in the field. You have full authority to deploy everyone however you need to, right, Tom?"

The mayor nodded then went back to holding his head in his hands. Poor guy looked totally overwhelmed. Not that she blamed him. This wasn't exactly the sort of thing you expected to have to deal with when you were sworn in.

"What if they don't believe me?" Lin asked.

"Tell them to call the Department and I'll have them busted down to traffic cop in the morning."

"I'll go too." Maria gasped as a fresh pain shot through her.

"No you won't." Her father came over and put his arm around her. "Outside the Department's wards I doubt you'd be able to stay on your feet, much less help."

"We'll direct any civilians in the area to come here," Lin said. "There's bound to be wounded. They'll need your help."

Maria clenched her jaw and nodded. They were both right. Her sensitivity to dark magic made her useless in a situation like this.

Lin rushed out of the office while her father returned to the phone. Sho helped Connie to her feet and turned to Maria.

"Let's go down and prepare. People will need places to lay down, blankets, and medical supplies."

"We have emergency gear in the Science Department as well," Connie said. Having something to do seemed to take her mind off Conryu.

Maria looked one last time out the window. The black pillar continued to grow in diameter and shadowy shapes flew out of it at random intervals.

* * *

The moment Conryu felt the dark magic surge he cast Cloak of Darkness. His desire to protect everyone caused the spell to cover the others in protective energy as well as himself. Jonny flinched and turned his head away. Kelsie moved behind him and buried her face in his back.

When the initial surge evened out into a mere gusher of power Conryu relaxed. A moment later the first shadow beast emerged, a crimson-eyed hound as tall as his shoulder. A blast of fire from Terra destroyed it.

"How do we close the portal?" Conryu asked no one in particular.

Terra shook her head and blasted another beast. "I have no idea. We need to capture Mercia alive so we can rip the information from her mind."

"Speaking of which, where'd the psycho run off to?" Conryu looked around, but found no sign of her.

"Master, I can sense her moving northeast."

"Go, I'll hold the monsters here." Terra hurled more flames. "Remember, we need her alive now."

"Right, I'll do my best. Prime, you're on point."

The scholomantic flew across the park and Conryu and his friends fell in behind. Take her alive, she says. It would be a wonder if he could stop her before she opened a second box.

"Master, there are ways to extract information even from a corpse. I can instruct you in the proper spell if it becomes necessary."

"Great. I'll be able to mark talking to a dead person off my list of creepy things to do. Any thoughts on how I might take her alive?"

"Your current spells are enough if you use them correctly. Blasting one of her legs off should take the fight out of her."

"Thanks, Prime, you're an inspiration."

They left the park and ran across a street filled with people gawping at the black pillar. Everyone was muttering and several terrified people clung to each other. He doubted they knew what they were seeing, but even the uninformed knew enough to realize it wasn't good.

Conryu forced people out of his way as he tried to keep up with Prime. It was a mark of how the nether portal transfixed everyone that a flying demon book didn't draw so much as a second look. He debated trying to herd them inside, but walls of stone and steel wouldn't slow shadow beasts.

Once they'd left the crowd behind, Conryu picked up the pace. It was probably more than Kelsie could handle, but he didn't dare take it any easier.

"Are we gaining, Prime?"

"Yes, Master. She's stopped."

"Shit! Where?" There was only one reason Mercia would have stopped and that was to open a second box.

"A hundred or so yards to your right."

He turned and sprinted, trusting his protective magic to stop any stray spells she might hurl his way. At the edge of the sidewalk a chain link fence stopped him cold. The light wasn't much better here and he could hardly see past the tip of his nose.

"Prime, where?"

"Keep going, Master, you're close."

There was probably a door in the fence, but he didn't have time to look for it. He focused his will on the fence. "Shatter!"

A whole section disintegrated into flecks of rust. He ran through the opening and promptly slammed into a crushed car. He must have entered a junkyard. Terrific, she could be hiding anywhere amidst all this crap.

He conjured a small fire globe and continued on. Jonny and Kelsie were somewhere behind him, but he didn't dare spare them a moment's thought. Hopefully they'd keep far enough back that he wouldn't have to worry.

A pool of sickly green light to his left caught his attention. He turned toward it, eager to catch up to Mercia.

"Careful, Master. That's necrotic light and it usually signals the presence of undead."

"Can you see in the dark?"

"Of course, Master. I'm a demon."

"Fly ahead and scout the area. I don't want to walk into another trap. And be careful."

Prime flew straight up and then towards the eerie light. Conryu closed his eyes and focused on his link with Prime. It took a moment, but then he could see through the scholomantic's eyes, though everything had a washed-out gray tone.

The light came from a huge mastiff with its head half severed from its neck. The undead dog didn't appear overly troubled by its current condition. It paced between two piles of crushed cars. That had to be where Mercia went.

"What's going on?" Jonny asked.

Conryu flinched and spun around. "Are you trying to give me a heart attack? I think we have a line on her. Wait here, stay behind the cars. I shouldn't be long."

He left his friends crouching behind the junk pile and snuck over toward the undead dog. At least he snuck as best he could considering he was standing in a pool of light in an otherwise dark night. Mercia couldn't have done much to the poor dog, there hadn't been time. He told himself that over and over as he approached.

He caught a glimpse of the mastiff at the edge of his light a moment before it charged. The zombie dog was slow and clumsy compared to the undead biker. He raised his hand, fingers crossed. "Break!"

The black orb flew out and struck the zombie square in the chest. It fell over on its side, truly dead once more.

That was too easy.

Familiar dark power washed over him as another pillar shot up into the sky to strike the bottom of the island. It expanded just like the first one and soon a pair of crimson eyes appeared in the dark, followed by another and another.

"All things burn to ash, Inferno Blast!" He swept his arm from left to right and burned the shadow beasts away.

"Master! She's fleeing west."

Should he stop the shadow beasts or pursue Mercia? Conryu wanted to tear his hair out. He couldn't be in two places at once. What was he supposed to do?

* * *

Shizuku hurled another lightning bolt into the undead monster's chest. So far she'd managed to burn its shirt off. Not the most promising results. She knew her light magic was weak against monsters like this, but she'd never imagined it being completely useless.

A boulder shaped from broken pavement slammed into the monster and staggered it sideways. Clair's magic was somewhat more effective, but not much.

"How are we going to stop it?" Shizuku asked.

"When Terra destroyed one she and Lin disabled it by blowing off its leg and burning the Faceless One inside to ash."

The undead regained its balance and stalked toward them again. Shizuku didn't have any magic capable of disabling the creature for more than a few seconds to say nothing about destroying its host.

She called a golden chain from behind it and yanked the monster back. Its dark magic nature degraded her spell in seconds.

A moment later a second pillar of darkness shot up into the night sky. Shizuku ground her teeth. They'd failed again to stop Mercia. Shadow beasts would be pouring out of that portal as well. They needed to wrap this up in a hurry.

"I think I can take off a leg, if you can burn away the shadow creature inside," Clair said as if reading her mind.

"No problem." If she could target the shadow creature directly, her magic would be much more effective.

Clair chanted and a chunk of the fire escape above them tore off with a high-pitched shriek of protest. The hunk of metal twisted and fused at her command, forming a blade which began to spin. With a sweeping gesture Clair sent it rushing in at the undead's legs.

The creature once again proved its agility, leaping over the spinning blade before coming crashing back to earth.

That didn't save it.

The instant the blade was past, Clair crooked her finger, calling it back. The second pass slashed the undead's leg off at the knee, exposing a twisted black leg inside.

"Light of Heaven burn away my enemies, Lightning Blast!" Without the flesh to provide insulation Shizuku's attack annihilated the exposed shadow limb.

The undead hopped and flailed, but could move no more than a foot or two per second.

Clair's blade came rushing in again, hacking off the second leg, and Shizuku again burned away the exposed inner limb. The stubborn creature attempted to crawl over to them.

The blade came flying down. It slammed through the undead's back, pinning it to the ground.

That steel blade gave Shizuku an idea. "Get back."

When Clair had moved a safe distance away she raised both hands to the sky. "Oh lord of the sky and king of Heaven, cast your might crashing down upon my enemy, Zeus's Lightning!"

Thunder cracked and a bolt of lightning that made her earlier attacks look like a stun gun hurtled down from the sky, striking the steel blade. Power crashed through the corpse, making the flesh translucent and exposing the bones. The energy burned away the Faceless One inside the body and the monster went still.

Shizuku bent over and gasped for breath. She fought the first hint of backlash that caused her vision to blur at the edges. That was the most powerful offensive spell she knew. If it hadn't worked she didn't know what they would have done.

"I know you're tired," Clair said. "But the others need us."

She straightened. "Let's go."

They left the alley and made the short trip to the first portal at a shuffling walk, which was all Shizuku could manage. When they arrived they found Terra frantically burning every shadow beast that appeared.

It was a losing battle. Even if she destroyed every one that appeared on the ground, there were black birds emerging higher up. The shadow ravens were spreading fast. They needed to close the portal before many more got out.

"How do we shut it down?" Clair cast a weak fire spell that burned away a shadow cat.

"No idea," Terra said between blasts. "I tried Dispel, but it absorbs dark magic like a sponge."

"If not dark magic, then what?"

"Maybe I can seal it with a ward?" Shizuku said.

"That much dark magic would eat through your spell in seconds." Terra grimaced. "I just don't see a way through this."

"If I maintain it by feeding a constant stream of light magic it might last longer, maybe ten minutes." That might have been way optimistic on Shizuku's part, but she was determined to do something.

"Then you collapse and get eaten by shadow beasts." Terra shook her head. "I can't allow that."

"You don't have a choice. If I can contain this threat you two can go help Conryu capture Mercia and maybe figure out how to close it permanently."

"Alright. I'll raise a wall of fire then you lay the ward. I know the chief was mobilizing the city's wizards. Hopefully someone will be along to help soon."

With Terra's spell destroying anything that tried to pass through, Shizuku began to chant and weave her ward, adding a silent prayer that she wouldn't pass out before she finished.

* * *

A chill ran through Lin when he gazed up at the second black pillar. The team had arrived near the portal in three cars and he'd immediately sent six officers armed with the magic guns out in pairs to patrol the area for shadow beasts. They hadn't seen any yet, but it was only a matter of time.

It didn't appear that the rest of the team was having very much luck bringing Mercia down. Shadow ravens, like the ones that attacked him and Terra down at the docks, flew out of the upper portion of the pillar. He drew a bead on an especially large specimen, more pterodactyl than bird, but lowered his weapon. It was too high and he didn't want to waste one of his precious magic bullets on a likely miss.

Lin and the other five cops headed straight for the second pillar. He'd noticed flashes of fire. Terra was fighting the invasion on her own and he didn't intend to let that stand.

"When we arrive, encircle the portal and shoot anything that looks like it's made of smoke. Be sure of your targets as there are friendlies and possibly civilians in the area."

Lin reached a chain link fence and began working his way around it looking for a gate. Beyond the fence, visible in the occasional flare of fire, was an auto junkyard. At least they didn't have to worry about damaging anything with stray rounds.

He hadn't gone far when he found a missing section of fence. He motioned two officers left while he took the other three with him to the right. Thirty yards in two figures huddled behind a pile of crushed cars.

Lin whistled. The two looked at him and he recognized Conryu's friends. That was two allies accounted for. He rounded another junk pile and there was Conryu himself, ten feet from the portal and busy burning everything that came within reach. There was no sign of anyone else.

It wasn't like seeing Conryu alive and well came as a disappointment, but where was Terra?

"Conryu!"

Conryu looked over his shoulder for a second at Lin. "Good timing, Sarge. Can you and your guys take over here? Mercia's getting away."

"We can hold them for a little while, go."

Conryu backed away from the pillar while Lin and his men moved in. The book flew down and hovered beside Conryu. The sight of the ugly thing sent a shudder through him.

"Don't get too close, Sarge. All that dark energy isn't healthy for regular people."

A shadow hound emerged from the pillar and Lin blew it away. "Don't worry about us, just capture the target."

Conryu collected his friends and jogged off after the book. Lin put them out of his mind and focused on the steady stream of dark monstrosities emerging from the portal. They didn't pour out in a gusher, but even at one every few seconds they'd burn through their limited supply of bullets in minutes. Once that happened, god help them.

* * *

Conryu hated leaving Sarge and the other cops on their own, but if he couldn't stop Mercia from opening that last box who knew what might happen. He'd hesitated for half a second about bringing Jonny and Kelsie with him, but they really wouldn't be any better off with Lin once the cops ran out of magic bullets. Not to mention they wouldn't have stayed even if he'd wanted them to.

"Where is she, Prime?"

"Not far away, Master. She's moving more slowly now."

"Why?" Jonny asked. "She's almost done. I figured she'd be rushing to finish the job."

"Mercia's expended a lot of power over the past half a day," Kelsie said between gasping breaths. "She has to be on the verge of a major backlash herself by now."

"Don't make assumptions," Conryu said. "Everyone's made assumptions about this woman and they've all been wrong."

Outside the junkyard the street lights were still working and apparently Mercia hadn't wanted to waste time or magic to douse them. That at least somewhat argued in favor of Kelsie's theory. He thought he saw a flicker of movement up ahead and muttered the vision-enhancing spell Terra taught him earlier.

It was Mercia, staggering up the street, the last box clutched to her chest. "There she is."

"Why doesn't she just open the stupid thing now?" Jonny asked. Conryu couldn't deny a certain amount of curiosity about that as well.

"Rituals are designed so that the key components must be in a particular formation for maximum effectiveness." Prime spoke like a professor giving a lesson. "Given that she has three boxes I assume she's planning to use a triangular formation. This box will no doubt go equidistant between the other two, forming the final point of an equilateral triangle."

"And if she succeeds?" Conryu wasn't sure he wanted to know and at the same time he needed to.

"Then the area between the three artifacts will become a single, giant portal allowing mass quantities of shadow beasts, as well as larger and more dangerous creatures from the netherworld, to enter the city. That would be exceedingly bad for the humans living here."

"No kidding." Conryu stopped and focused on Mercia. He had to risk taking her out from here. He honed in on her right leg. If he crippled her she wouldn't be able to move. "Shatter!"

A blast of dark energy raced toward the target. She must have sensed it as a counterblast negated his attack and she kept going.

"Shit! We're too far away." Conryu sprinted forward. Jonny kept pace, but the exhausted Kelsie soon fell behind.

"Master, I calculate she only needs another two hundred yards before she can activate the last artifact."

"I'm giving it all I've got." He barely had breath to speak. Mercia ducked between two dark businesses and out of his sight. "Son of a bitch!"

"She stopped, Master, and I sense power gathering."

Conryu lunged through the gap between the buildings. Mercia was bent over the box, making mystic passes over it.

He still had a chance.

Conryu focused all his will on the box. "Shatter!"

The dark wood exploded along with the gem inside and took at least one of her fingers with it.

"I got her!" Jonny lunged past him and leapt at Mercia.

Conryu caught a glimpse of her hateful expression and mumbled words of Infernal.

He concentrated on Jonny. "Cloak of Darkness!"

The spell came into being half a second too late. Jonny screamed and collapsed as the darkness covered him.

Mercia chanted a portal spell and disappeared through it. Conryu ignored the quickly closing disk and ran over to his friend. The Cloak of Darkness's effect vanished at his approach.

He knelt beside Jonny and checked his pulse, faint but still there. His bronze skin had taken on a pale, sickly hue.

"She's drained his life force." Prime flew down beside him. "Your friend should recover, but it will take time."

"*Should?!*"

"I'm sorry, Master, but without proper light magic healing nothing is certain with a spell like that."

He was going to kill that bitch when he got his hands on her.

"Conryu." Kelsie squeezed his shoulder and knelt beside him. "I heard what Prime said. I'm sure he'll be okay."

"I know he will, because you're going to stay with him. When Terra and the others show up, you tell them what happened and have Maria or her mom heal him."

"What about you?" She looked at him with wide, frightened eyes.

"I'm going after Mercia. She's the only one that knows how to close the portals." Conryu patted Jonny's chest and forced the tightness in his throat away. He was going to be fine. He had to be. "You'll take care of him?"

Kelsie nodded. "You can count on me. Go get her."

Conryu nodded, stood up, and opened a portal of his own. Cerberus was waiting and it was time to hunt.

* * *

Terra jogged toward the second portal with Clair in tow. She had to find Conryu and catch Mercia. She didn't care what Shizuku said, there was no way the exhausted wizard could maintain her ward for more than five minutes before backlash overwhelmed her. If that happened it was game over for the whole neighborhood.

The sound of gunshots and explosions reached her, but she couldn't pinpoint the origin. Terra frowned. She knew that noise. It sounded like Lin's enchanted pistol, only more than one. She picked up the pace. If Lin was fighting the shadow beasts then Conryu must have been incapacitated.

"How are we going to plug this one?" Clair asked as they ran.

"I'm open to suggestions."

"That's not what I wanted to hear. Say, where are all the wizards the chief was calling in to help? Seems like we should have run into at least one of them."

Terra shook her head. "You, Shizuku, and I are the strongest registered wizards in the city. We can't rely on any of the weaker casters to bail us out. If they can hunt down stray shadow ravens and protect the civilians I'll take it."

They reached a junkyard and at Clair's gesture the fence ripped apart. Terra glared at her, but she just shrugged. "I'm sure the owner has insurance and we're in a hurry."

It was a short trip to the edge of the portal. Lin and three other cops had the thing surrounded. There was no sign of Conryu or his friends. A fourth cop lay on the ground thirty yards from the portal. He'd been overwhelmed by the dark energy.

"Lin, what happened?" Terra asked. "Where's Conryu?"

Lin shot a shadow lion and it exploded. "He went after Mercia and left us to deal with the monsters. Man, I'm glad you're here. We're almost out of bullets."

Terra turned to Clair. "I can handle this. You go help Conryu."

Clair hesitated then nodded. "Which way did he go?"

Lin pointed to his left then returned his attention to the portal as the biggest shadow beast Terra had ever seen emerged in the form of a bear. He shot it twice before it exploded. "I'm out."

Terra raised her gauntlet-covered hand and chanted. "Flames of deepest crimson form a barrier to stop my enemies, Fire Wall!"

Enhanced by the power of the gauntlet, her barrier went all the way around the pillar and halfway up its height. An occasional shadow raven snuck out, but it stopped all the bigger beasts. The gauntlet would protect her from the effects of magical backlash, but only for a little while.

Hurry, Clair. She clenched her jaw and focused, determined not to let a single monster out.

* * *

Cerberus stopped and barked. As always there was nothing in the darkness that indicated to Conryu that this was where Mercia had exited, but he'd come to trust Cerberus's nose. If the demon dog said this was it, then it was.

He climbed down from Cerberus's back and cast the viewing spell. They were just outside a rusty warehouse on the waterfront. Why would she have come here of all places? At this time of night he wouldn't have to worry about any bystanders getting hurt. That was a small break.

"Be careful, Master. She may have left a trap."

Prime must have been reading his mind again. Conryu took a step back and found his view had shifted a hundred yards. That should be far enough.

He opened a portal and stepped through. When Prime had joined him he closed it and turned his attention to the dark warehouse. The windows were all blacked out so he had no idea where she might be inside.

"Reveal."

As expected, dark magic wards crackled around the outside of the building. He crossed his fingers and wrists. "Darkness dispels everything!"

The protections vanished under his assault.

* * *

Lady Raven emerged from the portal in her temporary living room. Damn the boy! He destroyed her final artifact and two weren't enough to complete the ritual. A pair of limited portals would be all they accomplished. Years of work down the drain. They might kill hundreds of people, if everything went well, but not nearly enough. She marched through the door and down the hall to where her last Faceless One waited. She was glad she hadn't brought all the undead with her, though she doubted this one would be any more effective than the others.

"I do not want to be disturbed." She stepped into her casting chamber and slammed the door behind her.

He'd be coming after her. There wasn't the least bit of doubt in her mind, especially after she'd nearly killed the other boy. Lady Raven had caught a glimpse of Conryu's face just before she fled. Yes, he'd definitely be coming after her. Hopefully her remaining guardian would be able to hold him off long enough for her to summon help.

Lady Raven snatched up her mask, tied it on, and entered the spell circle. Her thoughts went out to the others as she tried to get someone's attention. A shiver went through her when her wards were dispelled.

He was here already.

While she waited for one of her superiors to answer, Lady Raven focused her will on the spell circle and activated the emergency defenses she'd woven into it. They might slow him down at least.

The air grew hazy and Lady Dragon appeared. "You have failed."

"I opened two portals," she dared to point out. "The city will suffer. If Rennet had bought me a few more hours I'd have won."

"Blaming others for your failure is pathetic. However, you did partially succeed. If you can defeat the abomination I will allow you to retain your position as Sub-Hierarch."

That was at once far more generous than she'd dared hope and a mockery. There was no way she could defeat Conryu on her own. "Can you send help?"

"No. You succeed or fail on your own merit. The Society has expended all the resources on this that we can." Lady Dragon vanished.

She was truly on her own.

* * *

Conryu waited a second to make sure there were no delayed-reaction traps. When nothing happened he marched across the concrete toward the small side door. It was clear of magic and a quick inspection showed no other surprises. Still, better safe than sorry.

"Shatter!"

The door disintegrated and he stepped into the dark interior. A pair of fire globes appeared at his command and lit up the interior. It was a vast, empty space. He stepped inside and walked toward the center of the building. He found a round sewer access with the lid removed.

"Now we know why she used the sewer for her backup hiding places. But where is she now?"

"I sense someone above us, Master."

He turned his gaze to what appeared to be a collection of offices that looked down on the warehouse floor. It wouldn't be hard to convert those rooms into temporary housing and a workshop. He found a set of stairs leading up to the offices and jogged over to them. His boots clanged on every rung no matter how carefully he stepped.

"Don't be concerned, Master. I'm sure she sensed it when you broke her wards."

"Thanks, Prime. You really know how to reassure a guy."

The stairs ended in a rusty catwalk that led over to the office door. What sort of crazy manager would lay out his building like this?

Conryu studied the narrow path, checking for signs of weakness or traps. It looked clear, but just to be safe... "Cloak of Darkness."

He extended the spell to include Prime and set out across the path. When he reached the door without getting blasted or dropped to the cement below he let out a breath. So far so good.

Another spell disintegrated the door and he stepped into a living room. There was a couch, a pair of chairs and a coffee table with gossip magazines strewn across it. To his left was a set of French doors that led to a balcony. That area glowed with a combination of water and light magic which explained why he hadn't noticed it from the outside; it was hidden by an illusion. Straight ahead was another door that led deeper into the complex.

"I sense magic, Master. She's casting a spell."

Conryu ran across the living room and blasted away the door. A short hall led to a pair of doors, one to his left and a second straight ahead. Another of the zombie things stood beside the door on the left which radiated dark magic.

The undead did the trick where it leaned then charged toward him. Conryu was ready this time. He focused on the floor in front of it. "Shatter!"

He blew a hole in it just as the monster's foot came down. It fell through, but caught the edge with a massive hand. Conryu stomped down, smashing the brittle wood and sending the undead crashing to the floor below.

That should buy him some time. He threw his hand up and pointed at the door it had been guarding. "Break!"

The magic wasn't fazed so it must be coming from the room beyond. His next spell blew the door to splinters. On the other side was a Spartan casting chamber with Mercia in the center of a spell circle wearing a black mask.

He sent a spell at her leg, hoping to end the fight quickly, but the spell broke at the edge of the circle.

"Your magic can't penetrate my spell circle. We can keep each other company while this city dies." She cocked her head. "Either that or my Faceless One can tear you limb from limb when it arrives."

The undead's heavy tread on the metal steps was barely audible. He had at most a minute.

"Watch her."

He left Prime and Mercia facing each other and ran back to the living room. Through the doorframe he watched the monster step off the stairs and onto the catwalk. It spotted him at the same time and charged.

When it was halfway across he pointed at the steel walkway. "Shatter!"

A ten-foot chunk of catwalk disintegrated into flecks of rust and the undead went down. It wouldn't be coming that way again. Satisfied that there would be no more interruptions, Conryu returned to the casting chamber and found everything the way he'd left it.

"Where were we? I remember, you were about to tell me how to close the portals."

"No, I believe you were about to flail ineffectively against my spell circle."

She sounded so smug. He knew just the spell to wipe that grin off her face. "Deepest darkness twist and writhe. Grind and smash what I despise. Break through bonds and destroy all barriers, Death Spiral!" He twirled his finger and released the spell.

The protective shield resisted for a second before it blew apart. The spell continued on, annihilating the rear of the room and exposing the ocean beyond. Mercia fell to the floor and stared up at the ceiling, mouth partway open and drooling.

Conryu crossed the room in a second, knelt beside her, and slapped her across the face, knocking her mask askew. "Wake up!"

Mercia didn't so much as flinch.

"What's wrong with her?"

Prime flew down beside him. "Her consciousness must have been tied to the spell circle in hopes of making it stronger. When you broke one you broke the other."

"Fuck! How do we wake her up?"

"She may never wake up. If you kill her I can teach you a spell to capture her spirit and force it to tell you anything you want to know."

Conryu looked down at the unconscious woman. No one would blame him if he finished her off right now, not after everything she'd done. It wouldn't take much.

He wrapped his hands around her neck. Just squeeze, maybe break, her neck. She'd hurt Jonny. Maybe even killed him.

It would be so easy.

He let go, got up, and walked away. He couldn't just murder her in cold blood, no matter what she'd done.

"Let's have a look behind that last door. Maybe we can find something."

* * *

Kelsie knelt beside the unconscious Jonny and looked from him to where Conryu had disappeared into the portal. For a moment she wished she was Maria so she could do something to help Conryu's friend. She'd only known him for a little while, but he seemed like a nice guy.

She put her fingers to his neck like she'd seen them do on tv. His pulse was weak, but steady, the same as it was when she checked it a minute ago. Part of her wanted to pace while another part didn't dare leave Jonny's side for fear that the moment she did he'd die.

It was a ridiculous notion, almost as foolish as the overwhelming terror that filled her whenever she imagined Conryu's reaction if his friend died while she was taking care of him. The rational part of her knew he'd never blame her, but deep inside she wasn't sure. The thought of losing his trust and friendship made her stomach twist.

A chill ran up her spine. Something supernatural was nearby. She scrambled to her feet and looked around. Nothing was visible.

She looked up, and staring down at her with shining red eyes was a shadow raven. The creature was bigger than any natural bird outside of maybe a turkey. Its shape wavered like smoke in the wind, as if she needed another reminder that it wasn't a living creature she could scare away with a wave of her arms.

And that was about all she had to fight it off, strong language and gestures. Her magic certainly wasn't enough to accomplish anything. Kelsie flexed her fingers. Maybe she could hit it with a Shatter spell. When she'd teamed up with Conryu earlier they'd agreed that her magic had grown stronger.

Whatever happened she wasn't going down without a fight. The raven spread its wings and leapt from the roof. She focused on its head and forced all the doubts from her mind. This would work.

She raised her hand like she'd seen him do so many times. "Shatter!"

The shadow beast was knocked off course, its insubstantial body wavering as it fell to the ground. For a moment she dared to believe she'd done it, then the creature gave a whole-body shudder and spun to face her.

Its eyes were glowing brighter and she'd have sworn it looked angry. She moved between the grounded bird and Jonny. Kelsie pointed at it again.

Before she could cast, a fire arrow streaked past her and burned the raven away. She almost collapsed to her knees in relief. Clair stood in the mouth of the alley, a little wisp of smoke coming from the tip of her extended finger.

"Thank you." Kelsie knelt beside Jonny and checked his pulse again, not because she thought anything would have changed so much as to just do something.

Clair strode over, crouched down, and cast a light magic spell while passing her hand over Jonny. The school nurse had done the exact same thing to her when they returned from fighting the chimera so she knew what Clair was doing.

"Is he okay?"

"No, but he's not about to die either. Where's Conryu? Terra sent me to help him."

"I don't know. After Mercia did this to Jonny he went after her through a dark portal. They could be anywhere."

"Great. How am I supposed to help if I don't know where he is?"

* * *

Conryu disintegrated the last door, not so much because he needed to as because he wanted to burn off a little anger. It didn't help.

Beyond the doorway was a bedroom done all in black. The sheets, blanket, bed frame and cupboard were all painted glossy black. A quick glance didn't reveal anything beyond bad taste.

"Reveal." A section of the back wall glowed with illusion magic. That had to be something important. He pointed. "Break!"

The black sphere smashed the spell, revealing a niche with a large book bound in black leather. No wards protected it, which wasn't a huge surprise. In fact the bigger surprise was that she bothered with the illusion in the first place. If this was her home, even temporarily, it struck him as a waste of effort. It must suck being that paranoid.

He strode across the room and snatched the tome from its compartment. It had to weigh five pounds. Conryu threw it on the bed. It would take Maria a week to read a book that thick and he was way slower than her.

"Master, I can absorb the knowledge contained in its pages and summarize for you."

"Really?"

"Yes, it's a unique ability of demons like me. Shall I proceed?"

"Absolutely."

Prime landed on the book and dark energy flowed from him and into it. Conryu paced, arms crossed, and urged him to hurry. A minute later Mercia's book vanished and Prime grew an inch thicker.

"That was not a nice book, nothing there but black magic."

"You mean dark magic?"

"No. Well, yes and no. Yes, it's dark-aligned magic, but it's all spells and rituals that can only be used for vile and evil ends, primarily creating undead and nether spirits. A necromancer would—"

"What about the portals?"

"Right, once open they can only be closed from the inside or after the island has moved beyond their range."

"Great, you can tell me more on our way back." Conryu ran to the casting chamber with Prime right behind him.

When they arrived Mercia was still lying right where they'd left her. Conryu bent down, picked her up, and tossed her over his shoulder. He winced at the stench. She clearly hadn't bathed since her trip through the sewers, not that he was in much better shape. There was no sign of the undead thing and he had no intention of hunting it down. Someone else would have to take care of that.

He opened a portal and stepped through to find Cerberus waiting. He slung Mercia over the demon dog's back drawing a growl.

"I know, I don't like her either, but this is just temporary. I'll be back to collect her as soon as I can." He turned to Prime. "So how do I close the portals?"

Now that they had moved out of the normal flow of time he felt comfortable taking a minute to get a proper explanation.

"At the center of the pillar is a magic circle that maintains the spell. All you need to do is rub it away and the portal will instantly close."

"That's it? I don't even need to use Dispel?" If that was all he had to do he was going to feel exceedingly stupid for spending all this effort.

"That's it. However, to reach the magic circle you need to walk through a dense flow of pure dark magic. An ordinary human would be annihilated before he could even get within five feet of the pillar. I doubt even you'd survive entering it now that the portal has integrated with the island's magic."

Conryu clamped his jaw tight against a string of curses. "So there's no way I can get in there and turn it off? What about Cloak of Darkness?"

"A spell that weak wouldn't even get you through the first step. To even have a chance... Never mind."

"Don't give me 'never mind.'" He snatched Prime out of the air. "If you know something, spill."

"It's very risky, Master. It would be far more prudent to simply travel out of the city and wait for the spell to run its course."

He gave Prime a shake. "And sacrifice Jonny and Kelsie? Sacrifice Maria and her parents and my parents and god only knows how many strangers? How can you even suggest that?"

"I am your familiar, Master. Part of my duties are to do my best to keep you safe. Not strangers or your friends. You."

He spoke so calmly Conryu wanted to punch him in his scaly face, but it really wasn't Prime's fault. He was a demonic familiar, not the sort of combination from which you'd expect much sympathy.

"I appreciate your concern, but that's not a sacrifice I can accept. I'm going to walk into the nearest portal. The question is, are you going to tell me how I can have the best possible chance, or not?"

"As I said, I'm your familiar. If I can't persuade you to the most rational course, my next imperative is to help you survive your folly. The only spell that gives you even a fraction of a chance to live inside one of those pillars is called Reaper's Cloak. It literally summons a fraction of the Grim Reaper's cloak and wraps it around you. With the cowl up it should protect you from even the most powerful magic."

"Show me."

Prime opened and flipped to the proper page. "Remember, I said 'should.'"

* * *

Conryu stepped out of the hell gate fifty feet from the junkyard portal. He'd tried to open it closer, but the spell simply refused to function within that radius. The bottom half of the pillar was surrounded by a wall of fire which lit up the whole area. Terra stood well back, her gauntleted hand raised.

"Conryu." Lin jogged over from behind a pile of cars. "Did you get her?"

"Yeah, Mercia's with Cerberus, unconscious, but breathing. I know how to shut down the portals. Just in case I screw this up, it's been an honor to go to battle with you, Sarge."

He left the silently staring Lin and walked over to Terra. "I'm going to need you to open a gap for me."

"You can't go in there." The flames wavered when Terra spoke, drawing a grimace. "That much dark energy will kill you."

"Finally, someone who talks sense," Prime muttered.

"I can only shut it down from the inside. Unless you can maintain that wall of fire until the island moves out of range we don't have a choice. That would be, what, ten more hours?" Judging from the sweat pouring down her face he doubted Terra could maintain the spell for ten more minutes.

"Closer to fourteen. Alright, just tell me when."

He nodded and moved a short ways away. Conryu focused his will. If ever there was a spell he didn't want to screw up, this was it.

"I cannot go with you, Master. Reaper's Cloak only affects the caster. Just remember, we're still connected. If you need to draw on that link don't hesitate."

"Thanks, Prime." He blew out a sigh. Now or never. "Shroud of all things ending. Cowl of nightmares born. Dark wrap that looks upon the world's doom, Reaper's Cloak!"

The chill that enveloped him reached to his core. It wasn't physical cold, it was more like what ran through you when you knew someone was about to die. He raised his hands, reached back, and pulled the cowl up over his head. The world fell into black and white, all color and life washed away.

He didn't bother having Terra open a gap in the flames for him. Instead he simply strode over to the pillar and stepped through them. He didn't even feel warm.

Beyond the flames was a gap of several inches. A clawed length of arm thrust out into the fire and was quickly burned away. He tried to think of a good way to avoid those claws, but in the end there didn't seem to be any rhyme or reason to their appearance so he simple stepped out of the flames into the pillar.

The shock of cold caused his muscles to clench. He squeezed his eyes shut as every nerve in his body screamed with a single voice. If any of the shadow beasts struck him in passing he didn't register it over the overwhelming pain of just being in the portal.

He opened his eyes and kept moving. Only the knowledge that the longer he took the longer it would hurt allowed him to put one foot in front of the other.

Step by agonizing step he marched toward the center of the pillar. It couldn't have been more than ten yards across yet it felt like ten miles.

After five steps he reached a circle of runes spinning in the air. He didn't see them so much as become aware of them, since they were black against black. Some sense greater than sight told him where the runes waited.

Conryu trudged three more steps and swiped his hand through them. The spell dissipated instantly. It hardly seemed possible something so powerful was controlled by something so delicate.

The instant his hand passed through the runes the oppressive weight surrounding him vanished, yet the darkness remained. He looked around, but of course there was nothing visible.

After his second full turn he sensed something approaching, a powerful presence that made Lucifer feel like a child. He tried to flee, but was frozen in place. Not by fear, though he had enough of that, but rather by some force beyond his comprehension.

The presence grew stronger by the second and he soon figured out where it was coming from. He spun to his right and there it was, a figure carrying a scythe and wearing a shapeless black robe with a deep cowl. Like every other demon he'd encountered this one seemed to glow with its own inner light.

It stopped in front of him. The apparition was much taller than Conryu yet it appeared far less substantial. He held no illusions of what would happen should they come to blows. After all, it wasn't like you could fight Death.

"I have heard of you." Death's voice echoed, cold and emotionless. "You are the main subject of conversation of half the demons in Hell."

Conryu had no idea what to say and wasn't capable of speaking at that moment in any case.

"When you called my cloak I felt it. Your power is everything the others have claimed and more. I doubted, but having experienced it myself, I doubt no longer."

He needed to leave this place and close the second portal, but how did one bow gracefully out of a conversation with the Grim Reaper? "Thank you for the loan of your robe, sir. It saved my life and the lives of many others."

"It doesn't matter. All lives belong to me, sooner or later. And I don't loan my cloak. Only those with the power to seize it can do so."

A skeletal hand emerged from the fold of his robe and a finger crooked. Conryu's right arm rose of its own accord and the robe drew back, exposing his scarred forearm. The scythe rose. He tried to close his eyes, but found he was denied even that much control.

The gleaming blade swept down, passing through his arm like it was made of air. Conryu winced, expecting the limb to fall away. Instead what was left on his arm was a small mark that resembled the very weapon that had made it.

"I will be watching you, mortal. I expect you will provide me much amusement before I collect your soul."

The Reaper vanished and Conryu found himself standing in the middle of the junkyard.

Chapter 11

Finishing Up Sentinel

Conryu emerged, having closed the second portal, from what he hoped would be the last portal he had to open for a long time, in the Department parking lot. Dozens of cars jammed the lot, none of them resembling the pieces of junk the government employees usually drove. If he hadn't been so utterly exhausted he might have cared what they were doing there. As it was, all that mattered to him was that they were in his way.

He carried the still-unconscious Mercia like a sack of potatoes. Cerberus had been thrilled when he took her off his back. Conryu trudged the short distance to the front doors, shoved them open, and inside found a makeshift hospital set up with whatever supplies they had on hand, blankets, desks, chairs, you name it.

He spotted Maria right away. She was focused on a little girl with a shriveled right hand. She must have gotten grazed by one of the weaker shadow beasts.

"Drop the horrid woman, Master, and let's find you somewhere to rest."

That was the best idea he'd heard in a long time, but he couldn't just drop her and leave. If she woke up and escaped, the powers that be would probably want him to hunt her down again. Damned if he was going to provide an excuse for them to give him more work.

"Conryu!" Mr. Kane bustled over. He had his shirt sleeves rolled up and sweat dripped from his face. "You got Mercia."

"Yeah. Where can I stash her? She's getting heavy."

"Stick her in a chair and I'll find something to tie her up with. That's the best we can do for the moment." Mr. Kane went to find rope or whatever.

Conryu spotted a hard plastic chair near the wall and dumped Mercia into it. She slumped and tried to fall to the floor so he ended up having to hold her in place. That became a good deal more difficult when his mother tackled him from behind and started crying.

He couldn't make out what she was saying between sobs, but he assumed it was how happy she was that he was still alive. He would have loved to hug her back, but he lacked enough arms.

"Where's Dad?"

Mom gave one final sniff and let go. "Your father is helping move those too injured to walk. You know, more people were hurt trying to run from the monsters than anything. Lots of broken bones, bruises, concussions, that sort of thing. When the Department was announced as a safe zone they just started showing up. Poor Maria's been working nonstop."

He could relate to that. He finally spotted Mr. Kane returning with a pair of bungee cords. It had to be some sort of joke. At least they'd hold her in place, freeing him to lie down somewhere.

"Have you seen Shizuku?" Mr. Kane asked as he wrapped the cords around Mercia and the chair.

"She's okay," Conryu said. "But suffering from serious backlash. She maintained a light magic ward around one of the portals all by herself. It took a lot out of her."

"I'll be sure to fix her favorite breakfast when she wakes." He straightened up. "There, that should do for now."

Conryu forced himself not to shake his head. He'd locked his bicycle up better than that when he was ten. Right now all he cared about was finding somewhere to lie down before he fell down.

"Conryu." Maria had finally noticed him. She rushed over and hugged him.

He sighed and rested his cheek on her brow. This was why he'd pushed himself so hard. "Hey."

"What happened?" She stepped back but kept a grip on his hands. "Clair brought Jonny in and he's in bad shape. I did what I could, but he's going to be out of it for a while."

"It's a long story and I'm beat. How about I tell you tomorrow?"

"Deal." Maria kissed him and hurried back to help a woman with a deep cut on her forearm.

He smiled. She seemed to have found her place in all this chaos.

"Want me to drive you home?" his mother asked.

"God, yes, but first I need to check on Jonny. Did you see him?" As soon as he asked he spotted Kelsie sitting beside a glowing box. "Never mind. I'll just be a minute."

He picked his way through the people lying on the floor until he reached Kelsie. Her eyes were closed and she was snoring softly. He shifted his gaze to the box. Jonny's motionless form appeared here and there through the energy field. No way to tell how he was doing so he just watched his best friend breathe for a minute and sent him good thoughts.

"You're okay." Kelsie took his hand. "I was so worried. I stayed with him like you asked, but I was useless."

"No. Since I knew you were with him I could concentrate on dealing with Mercia. Thank you for that. I'm heading home. You want to come along?"

She looked from him back to Jonny. "Maybe I'll stay here for a while. I don't want him to be alone if he wakes up."

"That's sweet. I'll let his parents know where he is when I get home."

Conryu left her and rejoined his mother. He allowed himself a moment to hope Kelsie was transferring her crush to Jonny. It would be nice to have that off his plate at least. No doubt Maria would be pleased as well.

He hugged his mother. "Let's go home."

* * *

Conryu rolled out of bed at noon and debated going right back to sleep. His stomach snarled that it was time to rise and shine. He threw on jeans and a t-shirt before stepping out into the hall. He hadn't taken a step before voices, and not those of his parents, reached him.

No, one was his mother, the other Mr. Kane. Didn't he ever take a break? He probably needed sleep worse than Conryu. A couple steps brought Conryu to the end of the hall but kept him out of sight. Kelsie was lying on the couch. She looked at him, but he held a finger to his lips.

"Hasn't he done enough?" Mom asked. If it was possible to shout a whisper she managed it.

"I understand, Connie, but the mayor was insistent. He saved the city after all. The president also wants to offer him a commendation in Central. The whole Department of Magic will be there to observe."

Conryu bit his lip to keep from screaming. Why couldn't they all leave him alone?

"What if he says no?"

"They're not going to seize him at gunpoint, Connie."

"Really?"

"That was a complete misunderstanding. You have to make allowances for demonic interference. Remember, Conryu's a big deal, not just because of this, but because of what he is. A male wizard is beyond anyone's experience. That fact makes the people in charge nervous. Turning him into a hero is for Conryu's protection. The people need to view him as a protector and not a threat."

"Why would anyone see my son as a threat?" Dad asked.

"Because he's an unknown. And when something is unknown the default is to assume it's dangerous until proven otherwise. And, frankly, Conryu is dangerous, all wizards are. There's no way around that. But a dangerous hero, in the end, is better than the alternative. This isn't optional. The ceremony's tomorrow and the mayor expects him there, the Kincade girl as well. They're to be the stars of our little show. Please convince him, for everyone's sake."

A chair pushed back and a moment later Mr. Kane walked to the door and left. Fortunately he never looked Conryu's way.

"You can come out now, son." Of course Dad knew he was there.

Conryu nodded to Kelsie and walked around the corner. She sat up and smiled. "Morning."

"Afternoon actually, but whatever." He yawned and headed for the fridge.

"How much did you hear?" his mother asked.

"An awards ceremony, making me a hero so people won't be afraid of me." He emerged with cold pizza and two sodas. "Mr. Kane was right about one thing, I am dangerous. Did I tell you I took out a whole SWAT team with little more than a wave of my hand? If someone could tell me how to turn it off I'd take them up on it in a heartbeat."

Kelsie came over and joined them at the table. Her clothes were rumpled from sleeping in them. He handed her a slice of pizza and a soda.

"So will you do what the mayor wants?" Mom's eyebrows had drawn together and her worry wrinkle was twitching.

"Depends on exactly what he wants. And that business about the president is bullshit."

"Conryu!"

"It is. How much do you want to bet they want me to flush out anyone else that wormed their way into the Department in Central? I can imagine the argument now. 'You've already almost been killed a dozen times, why not be bait one more time? It'll save us all sorts of bother.'"

"You're too young to be so bitter." Mom gave his arm a squeeze. "Maybe it won't be that bad."

"Last time they had a gathering like this I was almost stabbed, so the bar is pretty low."

* * *

Conryu sat in the front while his mother drove and Kelsie rode in the back. Dad wanted nothing to do with the whole affair and went to the dojo this morning instead. If it had been up to Conryu he'd have gone with his father, but that might have been more trouble than it was worth.

He'd offered to let Kelsie sit up front, but she'd insisted she was used to riding in the back. Traffic was light as they made their way to the government plaza. He suspected everyone was still trying to come to terms with what had happened two days ago.

They pulled into the parking lot, but instead of going to the Department of Magic building they headed to the government offices. It made sense that they'd have the ceremony there considering the damage to the Department and the fact that the lobby was still full of injured people.

Jonny hadn't come out of his healing ward. His parents had called Conryu last night to let him know. They'd sounded pretty calm considering.

The parking lot of the government offices was packed, mainly with news vans. An elaborate stage with red-and-blue banners hanging from it had been built off to the right on a stretch of lawn. Cameramen were busy setting up while some poor worker attached the mayoral seal to the podium.

Mom found a parking spot and the three of them climbed out. Conryu stretched and yawned. He wouldn't have minded a little more rest, but the worst of the after effects had passed. Prime flew out beside him and spun around, taking in all the activities. Unless it was an emergency, Prime was under strict instructions not to talk any more than necessary.

They walked to the front doors, trying not to draw any attention. The circus would start soon enough, no sense in rushing things.

"Do you think I can get my cellphone back today? Maria said the cops took it when they came to our apartment." He scratched his head. "Maybe I should threaten not to go through with the ceremony unless they find it for me."

"Don't make trouble, Conryu. Let's just get this over with and go home," his mother said.

"If you play your cards right maybe they'll buy you a new one," Kelsie added.

Conryu did a quickstep and held the door for the ladies. "That's not a bad idea. They always talk about rewards at these things, a new phone is the least the mayor could do after he sicced the cops on me."

Mom went through first followed by Kelsie. He let the door shut and spun around. He hadn't been in this building since he took his driver's test two years ago. Nothing had changed. The floor had the same drab, white-and-black tiles, and the beige walls had faded to dirty white. The only thing missing was the bored woman that sat in the little kiosk and gave visitors directions to their department of choice. It looked like they'd shut the place down for today's carnival.

"Connie, Conryu!" Mr. Kane came around the corner from the elevators. "I'm glad you decided to come. Ms. Kincade, good to see you too."

"So how many hoops do I need to jump through before I can leave?" Conryu asked.

Mr. Kane winced. "It would be nice if you at least pretended to care about receiving the key to the city."

"I'll do my best. I'd be in a better mood if the cops would return my phone. It's probably sitting in an evidence locker somewhere, the battery getting lower all the time."

"That shouldn't be a problem. Now let's go. We need to get you two properly dressed and then there's the interview."

"What interview? No one said anything about an interview."

Mr. Kane couldn't look him in the eye. "It's not a big deal. Just a few questions from Kat Gabel."

* * *

"Are you kidding me?" Conryu raised his arms, sending the billowing black sleeves of the robe they told him to put on waving around. It had nonsense runes embroidered in silver thread on the cuffs and hem, a high collar, and gold buttons. It looked like a comic book version of a wizard's robe. "You want me to wear this ridiculous getup on national television?"

The slender, blond production assistant that presented him with the god awful thing shrank back. They were alone in a small, empty office that now served as a dressing room.

"Isn't that the sort of formal robe you guys wear?"

"No. I've never seen anyone wear anything like this outside of a low-budget movie." He pulled the robe off and handed it to her. "She can interview me in my regular clothes or we can skip the whole thing."

"Kat's not going to like this." The girl peeked at him from behind the robe.

"That's the best news I've heard all day." He maneuvered around the girl, grabbed the door, and yanked it open.

He stepped into the hall and blew out a sigh. Kelsie was in a different dressing room two doors up. Did they have her trying on something equally stupid or was this Kat's way of getting back at him for not doing an interview with her earlier? If it was the latter he was going to fry her cameras and microphone the moment he stepped into the interview room. Let's see her conduct her precious interview then.

He sensed Prime's annoyance coming from the room behind him. The blond girl had taken one look at his scholomantic and insisted he stay out of sight until after. Conryu opened the door and Prime flew out.

"If this is how they treat their heroes I'd hate to find out how they treat their villains," Prime said.

"I hear you, pal. It's only half a day here and another day in Central, then everything gets back to normal. Or at least what passes for normal in my life these days. If you'd told me last fall I'd be anxious to return to the academy I'd have said you were nuts. Now..."

The door to Kelsie's dressing room opened and she emerged wearing an outfit made up of thin black silk and gold chains. The outfit exposed both her legs to the hip, her flat stomach, and both arms. It was hot, but what on earth had they said to Kelsie to convince her to put on such a ridiculous outfit in the first place?

She spotted him standing there, looking at her, and Kelsie's face turned bright red. Conryu raised an eyebrow. "What's with the harem girl outfit?"

"They said it would look good with your robe. Um, where is your robe?"

"I informed the nervous young woman I wasn't wearing the gaudy thing and that if she didn't like it they could do the interview without me."

"And that worked?" She put her hands behind her back which pushed her boobs out tight against the material. She realized it at once and clasped her hands in the front.

Conryu looked down at his jeans and boots then back at Kelsie. "Looks like it."

"What if Kat has a fit? In my experience she likes things just so when she does a sit-down interview."

"You can't even begin to imagine how little I care what Kat thinks."

Kelsie frowned and marched back into the dressing room. Five minutes later she reemerged wearing the red dress she'd arrived in. "Better?"

"There wasn't anything wrong with the other one, I'm just not sure it was appropriate for national tv."

Their conversation came to an end when the door between the dressing rooms opened and Kat emerged wearing, he noted, a nice, professional blue suit. She looked them over and scowled. "Where are your costumes?"

"Hopefully on their way to the incinerator," Conryu said.

Kat rubbed her face. "Look, don't you know the news has to have an element of the dramatic if you want people to pay attention? We're trying to turn you two into something larger than life here. Think of it like being superheroes. Those are your costumes."

"Those are a variation on clown suits. I looked like a fool and Kelsie looked like someone dragged her out of A Thousand and One Nights. I'm through arguing. We can either do this as is or not at all."

Kat pursed her lips. "I was told you'd be cooperative. And what's that ugly book doing out of the conference room?"

Prime bared his fangs and Conryu was dearly tempted to tell him to bite her face off. "So you don't want to do the interview after all? That's fine."

He turned to leave and Kelsie hurried to join him. "This is an excellent bluff," she whispered.

"I'm not bluffing."

"Wait! Fine. You can wear your street clothes if you promise to answer all my questions."

"No deal." He kept walking. "I'll answer what I want or nothing at all."

He had almost reached the elevator when she said, "Okay."

Conryu winked at Kelsie and turned around. They rejoined Kat by the interview room door. "How long is this interview supposed to be anyway?" he asked.

"As long as it takes for me to ask all my questions. We'll edit it before it goes on the air tonight. Have a seat on the couch."

They went in and found Joe the cameraman fiddling with his tripod and pretending he hadn't been listening to the argument out in the hall.

"How's the leg?" Conryu sat on the left side of the couch so he'd be closest to the door.

"All healed up. I never got a chance to thank you for saving my life."

"No problem, though I'll admit sometimes I wish I'd let the snake eat Kat."

Joe's laugh drew a quick glare from Kat which shut him up. Kelsie sat beside him and Joe adjusted his camera.

"Is that any way for a couple to sit?" Kat motioned with her hands. "Snuggle up closer. Conryu, put your arm around her."

"We're not dating. Kelsie's my friend and if you suggest otherwise my actual girlfriend is likely to get pissed."

Kat stared at him for a moment as if trying to decide if he was serious. "I was told you were dating. My whole angle for this interview is you two as the new power couple in wizard circles. I mean the heir to the Kincade fortune and the only male wizard, how perfect is that?"

"Do I detect my mother's hand in this?" Kelsie asked.

"No, I swear. My information came from a source in the Department."

"If this is the same source that said I'd wear that stupid robe, you're going to have to find a better one."

"Ready when you are, Kat," Joe said.

She held her head in her hands. "I need a minute. All my questions are apparently based on horse shit."

* * *

Conryu and Kelsie left the pleasantly short interview and headed downstairs where they were supposed to wait for the ceremony to begin. It was a little strange walking through the empty hallways. He assumed all the workers were busy helping put the finishing touches on the platform.

"Who do you suppose told her we were dating?" Conryu had been thinking about it ever since Kat told them and he couldn't come up with anyone.

"If Kat's source is in the Department I'd bet my grandmother had something to do with it. What I can't figure out is why she'd bother. It's not like starting a rumor will turn it into reality."

"Why would she care in the first place?"

Kelsie shrugged and looked away from him. He frowned. She knew something, but apparently wasn't willing to share. He wouldn't push her. If she wanted to tell him eventually, fine, if not, well, that was her business.

"If it's any consolation, Master, I don't understand most of the things you mortals do."

"That makes two of us, Prime. It's not a good sign when demons start making more sense than people."

They reached the lobby and found a large group gathered. Conryu didn't know most of them, but he spotted Maria right away. She was standing with her parents looking out the doors and tapping her toe. She had on his favorite black dress and the silver jewelry she favored.

"Maria."

Her toe stopped and she spun around. "Where have you been?"

"Upstairs getting interviewed by my stalker. How's Jonny?"

"Still healing. My ward hasn't broken yet so he still has a ways to go. Mercia really drained a lot of his life force. He was very lucky to survive."

"I should have been quicker with that spell. Damn it!"

She took his hands. "It's not your fault. You did the best you could and I'm sure Jonny knows that."

Conryu pulled her into his arms and kissed her. "Thanks."

Over the top of her head he spotted Terra watching them with a strange twist to her lips. He couldn't read the expression, but it was one he'd never seen on her before. He put Terra's odd look out of his mind. Seeing her reminded him that he still had questions.

He sighed and released Maria. "Excuse me a minute."

Conryu caught Terra's gaze, and nodded off to the side.

She started moving away from the group and Conryu joined her. "So where'd you end up sticking Mercia?"

"She's in a temporary cell at the police station up the road. We put a spell canceller on so if she wakes up she won't be able to cast. She's going to be transported to the Lonely Rock at the end of the week."

"About the time we return from Central?"

"Just about then." Terra grinned. "When did you figure out we had problems in Central as well?"

"About the time I learned the succubus came from there."

Terra nodded. "Just to be safe let's discuss it when there are fewer people about."

"Alright, just one more question. Am I the bait or the distraction?"

"Distraction."

Well, that was better than being bait.

* * *

Conryu sat beside Kelsie on the over-decorated platform and listened to the mayor ramble on about what a close call it was and how they all had to pull together now, and blah, blah, blah. He leaned over and whispered, "You notice he didn't mention getting controlled by a demon and ordering the police to arrest an innocent man."

Kelsie swatted his shoulder, probably something she'd picked up from Maria, and held a finger to her lips. He sighed. He doubted any of the cameras were pointed his way at the moment, and certainly the microphones were unlikely to pick up his quiet comment. God, even being bait would be better than listening to this idiot for five more minutes.

"It is my pleasure to introduce the person most directly responsible for our victory two nights ago. Conryu Koda. Conryu, come up here and say a few words."

There was a smattering of cheers when he stood and walked over to the mayor like they'd told him. He shook the proffered clammy hand and restrained a grimace of distaste.

"Just stick to the script," the mayor said before taking his seat directly behind the podium.

He stepped up to the microphone and looked out over the faces and cameras staring at him. An overwhelming urge to turn and run hit him in the gut. He fought it down, squeezing the sides of the podium until his knuckles turned white.

They'd left a prewritten speech for him. He glanced at the paper. It opened with him thanking the mayor for his brave leadership and became stupider from there. No mention was made of all the efforts his friends had made or that Jonny had almost died.

He couldn't read it, not if he wanted to be able to look at himself in the mirror in the morning. "Thank you for the warm welcome. I'm sure one of the mayor's fine speechwriters worked really hard to get this ready for me, so I want to apologize in advance for ignoring it." That drew a nervous laugh from the crowd.

"Anyway, you've all heard a lot about what I did and how Kelsie helped me, and she did, I couldn't have succeeded without her. What you haven't heard about is all the other people I couldn't have succeeded without. Most of them are right here in the front row. First and foremost is Terra Pain and Clair Tines, they're the Department wizards assigned to this city. The two of them, along with Detective Lin Chang have worked for a year on this case. Without them I wouldn't have had a clue what to do, so give them a round of applause, they certainly earned it."

The crowd seemed a little confused, but obliged him by clapping. Terra looked like she wanted to strangle him and Clair's cheeks had turned bright red. Conryu didn't know where Sarge was, but hoped he was equally embarrassed.

"Next comes the three most important people in my life after my parents: Mr. and Mrs. Kane, along with their daughter Maria. Mr. Kane is the Department chief and he's worked every bit as hard as his subordinates. Mrs. Kane singlehandedly held off the shadow beasts from one of the pillars; if not for her many more people would have died. And of course Maria, who worked herself to exhaustion healing people injured in the chaos. The three of them are family to me and I wouldn't have been able to do any of the things I did without their support."

The cheers came unprompted this time. The mayor's chair creaked as he started to rise. Conryu had no intention of going anywhere until he finished. They wanted him to give a speech and he meant to finish it.

"Last, but not least, I need to mention someone who couldn't be with us today. My best friend Jonny Salazar was nearly killed by the lunatic that caused all this mess. Jonny's going to be okay, but he hasn't woken up yet. If you'd send him your well wishes I'm sure his family would appreciate it. Thank you."

Conryu turned, nodded to the mayor, and marched off the stage. Kelsie jumped up and hurried to catch him. "I think they call what you just did, muddying the narrative."

"I call it telling the truth. If they didn't want to hear it, they should have had someone else speak."

Chapter 12

Central Spy

Conryu looked out the window as the scenery whizzed by. It was getting late. The plan was to travel through the night and arrive first thing in the morning. When he left the academy he hadn't intended to be on his way back to Central so soon.

He and Kelsie sat alone in a luxury cabin, Maria having not received an invitation to this get-together. Everything was leather, hardwood, and silver, including a little tray with snacks. He thought the private carriage they insisted he use when he went to school was nice, but this was over the top. It said something that Kelsie hadn't even batted an eye when they boarded three hours after his speech. At least they'd given them a chance to pack a change of clothes.

Terra and Clair were riding separately in the hopes that they wouldn't be noticed. Judging by the amount of press that had seen Conryu and Kelsie off they'd gotten their wish. He doubted a single person noted the two women getting on board with the other passengers. He'd hardly recognized Terra when she showed up in street clothes instead of her usual gray robe.

He'd tried to pry more information about their plan from the two women, but he hadn't gotten much beyond the fact that they couldn't tell him in case he ran into the spy at headquarters. Conryu figured they were still annoyed he mentioned them at the ceremony.

"Penny for your thoughts," Kelsie said when the silence had stretched for an uncomfortable length.

"Just wondering what sort of craziness we'll be drawn into this time. What do you think your grandmother will have to say?"

She grimaced. "I'm not looking forward to finding out. Disobedience isn't well received in my family."

"From what I can tell nothing is well received in your family. Maybe they'll send some more thugs to grab you. I wouldn't mind an old-fashioned fistfight after all the magic."

"I doubt it. There'll be more press waiting when we arrive and we're traveling in the presidential limo as a sign of gratitude. Mom wouldn't want to make a scene with so many people watching."

Conryu settled deeper into the buttery leather. "Probably just as well. You should try and sleep. I'm beat."

He pushed the recliner back and closed his eyes. Prime would keep a lookout so he wasn't worried on that score.

The ringing of the cheap flip phone he'd been using woke him some time later. He blinked the sleep from his eyes and dug it out of his pocket. The little readout on the front said midnight. What did she want this late at night? Maria was the only one who had this number.

"Yeah?"

"Jonny woke up and he's fine. A little weak and a lot hungry, but otherwise fully recovered."

A weight lifted off his chest. "That's awesome. Tell him I'll see him in a day or two. And thanks for calling."

"I knew you'd want to know right away. How are you and Kelsie doing?" She didn't even sound jealous which amazed him.

Conryu glanced at the softly snoring Kelsie, a little drool pooled under her cheek. "We're good. Happy to be bored for a few hours. I'm afraid it won't last."

"I fear that too. Be careful."

"I'm always careful."

"Says the guy that walked into two portals to the netherworld. I mean it, Conryu."

"I know. I love you."

She was silent for a heartbeat. "Love you too."

He hung up and grinned. Jonny was awake and okay. That was the best news imaginable.

* * *

The train stopped in the Central City station just as the sun was rising. The dazzling sunrise reflected from thousands of windows was breathtaking. He'd lost track of the fact that there were beautiful things in the world amidst all the madness. It was nice to get a reminder once in a while.

Kelsie groaned and rubbed her eyes. She'd slept the whole way. Conryu wished he could say the same. After Maria's call he'd mostly tossed and turned. His joy at knowing Jonny was awake and well made up for it. He felt like he could fly without magic.

"I dreamed the phone rang last night," Kelsie said.

"It did." He told her about Jonny. "His parents must be so relieved. He's an only child, same as me."

She smiled and attempted to fix her hair with her fingers. "Me too. I'm going to wash up."

Kelsie went to the small bathroom and closed the door, leaving him alone. They'd be getting off soon so he wouldn't have time to clean up. Luckily his short hair didn't need much attention. A shower would be great though.

Fifteen minutes later they were standing on the platform along with all the other passengers. A quick scan of the area revealed a man in black holding a sign with his last name on it. Conryu pointed him out and he and Kelsie strolled over. He'd kept Prime in his bag so as not to draw too much attention. It appeared to be too early for the press to be up.

"Conryu Koda?" the man in black asked.

"Yup."

"You look taller on tv."

He shrugged, not certain how to respond to that. "So where are we headed?"

"The director has arranged a hotel room where you can prepare for the meeting with the president which is scheduled for ten o'clock."

"Great." Conryu gestured toward the exit. "Lead on."

They made their way through the crowd and out the door. Waiting at the end of a flight of steps was a black limo with the Alliance flag—ten stars set in a circle on a blue rectangle—on the side. The driver held the door for them and he and Kelsie piled into the back along with their small bags. The door shut and a minute later they were off.

Conryu was too nervous to care about the city outside the tinted windows. Was four hours going to be enough time for Terra and Clair to track down the spy? He hoped so, but it seemed pretty iffy. They'd spent most of a year trying to find Mercia and had come up empty.

"You seem a bit tense," Kelsie said.

Conryu realized he'd sunk his fingers an inch into the leather-covered armrest. "Sorry. We're so close to the end of this and I'm afraid something's going to go wrong."

"That's understandable, since nothing's gone especially right since I met you. Try to bear in mind that you already saved a whole city. Surely you can handle a press conference and shaking hands with the president."

He hadn't told Kelsie the real purpose of their visit and he wasn't sure if anyone else had. Either way, he didn't plan on discussing it in an unsecured location with a guy he didn't know an arm's length away. They passed the rest of the trip in silence and ten minutes later the car stopped in front of a thirty-story bronze-faced hotel called The Luxury Arms. He'd never heard of it, but that didn't mean anything.

Kelsie had a bright smile as they climbed out of the car. Conryu grabbed both bags without thinking about it. Hers didn't weigh enough to say so thanks to the magic.

The driver slammed the door. "I'll be back to pick you up at nine thirty. Please be waiting in the lobby."

When he'd gone they started for the revolving door. "Do you know this place?" he asked.

"I've never been here, but my family owns it. I think Mom meets her boyfriends here when she's in the mood."

"Well, it's a nice place for it."

They pushed through the door and entered a lobby done up in polished brass and warm hardwoods. A collection of leather chairs sat in a clump to one side. A pair of men sat reading newspapers and drinking coffee. On the opposite side was the check-in desk.

Kelsie walked over like she owned the place, which was appropriate. Conryu followed, feeling a good deal more out of his element. It took only a moment when they told the brunette behind the desk their names to get a key and head up to the president's suite.

"Is that gold?" Conryu asked when they reached the suite door. It had designs inlaid in the shiny yellow metal.

"Yeah, this room is ten thousand dollars a night after all. The guests expect the best." Kelsie unlocked the door and pushed it open.

Sitting on the bed waiting for them was Malice Kincade.

* * *

Terra hadn't gotten used to working without her gray robes. How long had it been since she went anywhere in slacks and a blouse? Too long, if she was honest with herself. She flexed the fingers of her right hand. The gauntlet was back in storage and she found she missed its reassuring presence. That and her magic was so much weaker without it. Just as well she didn't get used to it. Magical artifacts risked becoming a crutch if you came to depend on them too much.

Out of the corner of her eye Terra noticed Conryu and Kelsie leaving the station. She'd never admit it, but she wished they could have brought him along on this job. Conryu had proven himself both reliable and powerful. Especially powerful. When he donned the Reaper's Cloak and walked through her wall of fire like it was nothing her heart had skipped a beat. Those flames had been nearly two thousand degrees. Not to mention what entering a nether portal would do to a normal person.

Clair gave her a shake. "Time's wasting. Where are we meeting her?"

"A coffee shack two blocks north." Terra hitched her carryall up higher on her shoulder. It shouldn't take more than a minute or two to walk it.

The worst of the crowd had cleared so they had no trouble making their way down the steps and up the sidewalk. Cars clogged the road, horns honked, and several people shouted obscenities. Terra hated Central, everyone was so rude. It was like they thought living in the capital gave them the right to be jerks. With any luck she and Clair wouldn't be here more than a day.

They had no trouble finding the coffee shack. Sitting at a small table out front, sipping coffee and nibbling a croissant was a young woman in a bright red dress, holding a large leather purse on her lap. She fit the description they'd received perfectly. Terra's instructions were to make contact, collect the artifact, and say nothing about their mission.

She walked right up to the girl in red. "Evelin?"

The girl put down her snack and looked up. "Yes. Terra?"

"That's right. You have something for me?"

Evelin dug a package wrapped in plain brown paper out of her bag and handed it over. "Dean Blane never said what I was carrying."

The unspoken question lay between them, but Terra just accepted the item and nodded. “Thanks.”

Evelin shrugged. “I guess I don’t need to know. Good luck with whatever.”

Terra tucked the item into her carryall, nodded again, and set out down the street. They needed to find a quiet place to perform the ritual.

“Do you know a good place?” Clair asked. She’d been quiet during their meeting with the courier, which was unlike her.

“No, I haven’t been to Central since I joined the Department, right after graduation. Do you? You grew up here after all.”

“I think there’s a park up the street aways. If it’s the one I remember there’s a bandstand and a thick clump of spruce. Either spot would offer a little privacy.”

“Sounds perfect. How do you know about it?” She glanced at Clair whose cheeks were a little flushed.

“My boyfriend and I used to make out in the bandstand when we were in high school.”

“I didn’t know you had a boyfriend.” Clair had never spoken much about her life outside the Department and Terra was just as happy with things staying that way, but for some reason this mission felt less official than their work back in Sentinel City.

“He dumped me after I passed the test. Didn’t want to date a wizard I guess. Made me a little wary of men in general.”

Terra understood that. It was hard to find a man that understood the pressures of being a Department wizard, always on call, working long hours, hunting down dangerous wizards.

When she had a free moment Terra allowed herself to imagine a relationship with Lin, but she never did anything about it. Maybe when this business was finished. She wasn't getting any younger after all.

"Here we are."

She'd been so wrapped up in her thoughts Terra hadn't even noticed the neatly trimmed park that appeared in front of them. It was a nice spot, not overly large, with a fountain in the center. She spotted the green-and-white bandstand not far from the fountain. It was way too exposed. If anyone passing by noticed their casting and called it in they'd draw attention better avoided. The thick stand of spruce near the northeast corner looked ideal.

"Let's use the trees."

Clair led the way. As they approached she muttered a spell and the branches swayed out of their way. The sun hardly reached them in the center of the grove. If they'd wanted to use dark magic it would have been an ideal spot.

When the branches were back in place and obscuring them from view Terra pulled out the parcel and unwrapped it revealing a battered and bent, formerly white mask. She handed it to Clair and pulled out the black mask they'd seized from the still-unaware Mercia.

It hadn't taken Terra more than an hour to figure out the mask was a type of communication device. Once she knew that she'd called the school and discovered they'd dug a second one out of the sorority building's rubble. With the two items in their possession it should be a simple matter to track down the spy.

When they'd gotten as comfortable as possible under the circumstances Terra asked, "Ready?"

Clair nodded and they began to chant.

* * *

"Grandmother?" Kelsie couldn't have been more surprised. She'd hoped for some time alone with Conryu, not that she expected anything to happen, but a girl could dream. "Why are you here?"

Her grandmother's expression pinched even tighter. "We need to talk before your meeting with the president. There are certain protocols and we've prepared a short speech for Conryu."

She glanced at Conryu who'd put the bags on the second bed. He didn't seem especially surprised or put out to find someone waiting in their room.

"It would be nice," her grandmother continued, "if he stuck to it."

Conryu grinned. Kelsie couldn't believe he had the audacity. "If it's more nonsense like they wanted me to read yesterday, don't get your hopes up."

The only sign of Grandmother's displeasure was a slight deepening of the wrinkles around her eyes. "Don't worry, it's only a few paragraphs thanking the president for the medal and how honored you are to receive it."

"That's fine, I guess. You two probably want to catch up. I'm going to hit the shower." He strode off through a side door and closed it behind him.

Kelsie stared for a moment, wishing she had the guts to do something like that. When she turned back her grandmother was scowling even fiercer than usual.

"What a troublesome young man. Why couldn't someone more tractable have been born with his power?"

Kelsie knew she didn't actually want an answer. "So there must be something more important than discussing protocol that brought you out here."

"I had hoped that by coming myself I'd impress upon him the importance of behaving today." Grandmother cocked her head when the shower turned on. "Have you made any progress getting him into bed?"

Kelsie was struck dumb for a moment. She couldn't believe her mother had shared the details of her plan with anyone else. And that Grandmother would bring it up with Conryu just yards away, even if he was in the shower, was unbelievable.

"No. As I tried to explain to Mother, he doesn't like me that way. We're just friends."

Grandmother snorted. "I suspect if you'd walked into his bedroom naked, nature would have taken its course. He's just a man after all. What was the point of you going home with him if you weren't planning on carrying out your task?"

"Maybe I just wanted a couple weeks away from Mother," she dared to say.

"Speaking of your mother, she expects the two of you for dinner tonight. Her exact words were that since Conryu was kind enough to host you at his home the least she could do is return the favor."

Kelsie grimaced. She hated the thought of exposing Conryu to her horrid home life. That said, she wasn't sure she dared to disobey her mother a second time so soon after the first. If it was just one night it might be okay.

"I'll be sure to tell him."

"That's better." The water stopped and Grandmother changed subjects. "Have you been briefed on the second reason for your visit?"

"I wasn't aware there was a second reason."

Her grandmother gave a short explanation of the hunt for the spy. "We're hoping his arrival will draw the spy's attention so we can take her by surprise. Either that or she attempts to murder him and we can catch her in the act. Our hunters are in motion as we speak."

Conryu emerged from the bathroom wrapped in a fluffy white robe. He shook his head, sending drops of water flying. "The faucets are plated in gold, the shower head too. Did you two have a nice chat?"

"Wonderful." Grandmother went to the door. "I'll see you at the ceremony."

When the door had closed Conryu settled on the bed across from her. "So what's this about getting me into bed?"

Kelsie almost choked. "How could you have heard?"

His bag thrashed around. Conryu unzipped it and Prime flew out. "Isn't spying one of the things a familiar is supposed to be used for?"

She'd forgotten all about the scholomantic. "Did you go off on purpose to find out what we'd talk about?"

"No, I really needed a shower. Though I trust your grandmother about as far as I can throw Cerberus, so a little spying seemed in order. Now stop trying to change the subject."

She sighed. There was no way around it short of telling him it was none of his business which it clearly was. "Mother had the brilliant idea that I should convince you to sleep with me so we could add your genetics to the family bloodline. It's something of a Kincade obsession, constant improvement through selective breeding. Mother selected my father after exhaustive genetic research. Adding the DNA of a male wizard is simply irresistible to her."

"So she ordered you to sleep with me in hopes of getting it." He shook his head, disgust twisting his features. "I know I've said this before, but your family sucks. It'll be interesting to see how dinner goes."

"You mean you'll go?" She couldn't hide the surprise in her voice.

"Sure. It's my fault you're in trouble for disobeying. I'll do the best I can to get you out of it, short of sleeping with you that is."

"Would it be so terrible?"

He shook his head. "No, I'm sure it would be fantastic. Then I think of the look on Maria's face when she found out." He shrugged as if there was nothing more to say.

And there wasn't. She realized that. No matter her silly fantasies, he loved Maria and would never do anything that might hurt her.

Maybe one day she'd find someone that loved her that much.

* * *

Terra's consciousness drifted as she sought the connection between the three masks. She held Mercia's in her hands and across from her Clair held the battered mask recovered from the academy. The link between them was weak despite their proximity. That meant finding one even further away would be that much harder.

She needed to focus. She breathed deep of the sweet scent of the trees then blocked it out. Clair's chanting of the ritual spell faded until she was completely unaware of it. The hard ground under her and the pebble poking her thigh vanished from her perception.

All that existed for her was the magic connecting the masks. She constructed an astral avatar and set it loose from her body. With her consciousness now fully freed from its physical host she turned her attention to the thin trail leading up and away from the clump of trees and into the city.

She brushed it with her invisible hand, willing the energy to glow brighter. Under her coaxing the link grew stronger, strong enough to follow. Her avatar flew along beside the tendril of magic. It took all her skill to keep the flow of energy smooth and unbroken. Time was of the essence, but if she rushed it would require her to return to her body and try again, which would take even longer.

So she was forced to creep along. She lost all awareness of time, her entire being focused on maintaining the trail. Eventually it led her to a tall apartment building. When Terra tried to follow the energy inside she hit an invisible ward and was unable to pass.

That shouldn't have surprised her. Many buildings, certainly all the ones in the better parts of the city, had barriers to prevent supernatural entities from entering. It was a basic security precaution in the capital.

Unable to continue pursuit in her incorporeal form, she flew down and hovered in front of the entrance. She memorized the address and willed her spirit to return to her body.

She blinked and opened her eyes. "I found her, or her mask at any rate. How long was I gone?"

Clair fell silent and checked her watch. Her eyes widened. "It's nine-thirty. Half an hour to the speech."

Terra scrambled to her feet, the stiff muscles in her legs complaining about the rough treatment. "The spy's apartment is halfway across town. This is going to be close."

They left the spruce grove and hurried to the sidewalk. Clair raised her hand and let out a shrill whistle when a cab appeared. The yellow car pulled over and the women got in.

"The Sky Bride complex and step on it," Terra said.

The cabbie squealed his tires when he pulled away from the curb and they raced down the street. They hadn't gone more than a hundred yards when they hit the first red light. Terra glared up at the indifferent street light wishing she knew a spell to control electronics. Not that there wasn't one, she just didn't know it.

The light changed and they were off. They hit three more red lights before reaching midtown. Clair checked her watch. "Fifteen minutes."

"Come on, come on." Terra tapped her finger on the window in rhythm to her racing heart. She did not want to have to rely on plan B which was hoping the spy tried to kill Conryu and thus reveal herself.

With five minutes to spare the cab pulled up in front of the building Terra had visited in her astral state. She threw the cabby a fifty and they raced into the building without waiting for change.

When they entered the lobby a middle-aged man in a uniform sitting behind a desk to their right said, "Can I help you ladies?"

"We're looking for someone. It's Department of Magic business." Terra pulled the raven mask out of her bag.

"Got any ID?" the guard asked. "Cause if you don't I can't let you through."

Terra glared at him. "Winds rage and howl, crush all who stand in my way, Gale Burst!"

A focused gust of wind picked the guard up and slammed him into the wall behind his desk. He slumped to the floor with a groan and didn't move.

"That may have been rash," Clair said.

"We're in a hurry." Terra reestablished her psychic link with the mask. The moment she did the line of magical energy appeared, thicker and stronger than before. "This way."

Terra ran to the elevator and hit the button for the top floor. As they rode up she watched the line of energy. When it went horizontal she hit the emergency stop. "This floor."

Clair muttered a spell and flicked her wrist. The elevator doors slammed open. They were a foot above the floor, but Terra just hopped down. Happily there were no tenants out in the hall to witness the two crazy women leaping from the stopped elevator.

She resumed following the line of magic. It led to a closed door sealed with a light magic ward. A quick analysis revealed that it was cast by a different wizard than the one that did the spirit ward surrounding the building. "This has to be it. Do you want to break the ward?"

"The spy will know we're coming."

"Do you have another plan? If you don't we're out of time."

"Okay." Clair broke the ward and blasted the door off its hinges.

Terra rushed in to the immaculate apartment. No one attacked them and she didn't sense any other magic. She followed the mask's link to a table beside the bed. In the drawer was an identical mask done in blue feathers.

"I'll call it in," Terra said. "Look for anything with her name on it."

Clair set about searching while Terra dug her phone out. She dialed the Central division's number and after three rings a secretary answered. "Department of Magic, how may I direct your call?"

"I need to speak to Director Kincade immediately, it's an emergency. My name is Terra Pane, ID number six three one one two. She's expecting me."

Faint tapping like on a keyboard was followed by, "I'm sorry, the director isn't in her office and her cell phone is turned off. Would you like her voicemail?"

Leaving a message wouldn't do any good. By the time the director checked it the event would be over. "That's not going to work. I need you to run this to her yourself."

"I'm sorry, Ms. Pane, but we're operating on a skeleton crew right now since everyone has gathered in the briefing room to listen to the president's speech. I can't leave my desk."

Terra wanted to scream. Clair came into the room and handed her a paper with a name on it. "Listen to me. Alyssa Warren is a spy and may attempt to kill Conryu Koda during the address. If you want to accept responsibility for not alerting the director, that's up to you, but I suggest you think hard about it."

The sound of a receiver hitting the desk was followed by silence. She'd done everything she could. Terra hoped it would be enough.

* * *

They called the area where the president intended to give his speech "the briefing room" and it was the only one in the building big enough to hold everyone. Conryu looked out over all the faces staring back at him and wondered if one or more wanted him dead. No one had told him anything about the spy getting captured and judging by the extra tightness in her face, Malice hadn't heard anything either.

In addition to the audience watching, there were two cameras trained on the podium. When the ceremony began they'd broadcast the speeches live all over the world. He dearly hoped that this would be the last time he had to be on tv for a while.

Malice sat beside Kelsie in one of the three chairs set behind the podium facing the room. They were waiting for the president to arrive. Apparently he was behind schedule. When you were president you could run late without worrying about anyone complaining. Must be nice.

He glanced to his right. Prime flew near the ceiling just out of sight. He took a deep breath to calm his racing heart. Whatever was going to happen, he'd be ready to deal with it.

Beside him Kelsie was chewing her lip and twisting a ring on her finger. She'd been horrified when she realized he'd listened to her conversation with Malice and he regretted, at least a little, that he'd spied on them, but he needed to know what was going on around him too. The fact that she hadn't done anything to further her mother's plan made him inclined to keep trusting her.

Music blared and a voice said, "Ladies and Gentlemen, the President of the North American Alliance."

Everyone rose and offered polite applause. A moment later the president entered stage left. He was a fit man with steel-gray hair and dressed in a crisp blue suit. He walked straight up to Conryu and held out his hand. Conryu gave it a firm shake. He met the sharp green eyes without flinching.

The president offered the hint of a smile. "Nice to meet you, young man. Malice tells me I have you to thank for saving one of my cities."

"Me and many others, sir."

He broke into a full smile. "Yes, I caught your speech along with Tom's complaints. I trust you won't feel the need to register your feelings a second time."

"No, sir."

"Excellent." The president clapped him on the back and stepped up to the microphone.

He raised his hands and the room fell silent. "Thank you everyone, please take your seats."

Everyone sat save one woman, a slender wizard wearing a billowing gray robe. He guessed she was in her mid thirties. Her eyes glared at the stage, hard and cold as ice.

The president cocked his head. "Did you want something?"

Conryu got a sick feeling in the pit of his stomach.

"Yes." The wizard raised her hand and something flashed. "Your head."

He tried to cast a protective spell, but he was too slow. A blinding flash scrambled his brain and sent him crashing to the floor along with everyone else in the room save the spy.

Conryu blinked, trying to clear the spots from his eyes. The president lay on the floor a little ways away, twitching.

He sensed Prime getting ready to attack, but sent negative thoughts. The scholomantic wouldn't have a chance against a wizard.

Conryu managed to roll onto his back and found himself staring up into the twisted face of the spy.

"So you can still move a little," she said. "I'd heard the reports of your power, but I assumed they were exaggerated to make the failures of others more palatable. You just lie there. Once I deal with the president, you're next."

She turned away and Conryu racked his brain, trying to force his thoughts into some kind of order. The spy chanted and a shining white blade appeared in her hand.

"No." He gasped the word out.

She turned to look at him, her lip curling in a sneer.

Conryu turned his full will on the spell in his mind. "Shroud of all things ending. Cowl of nightmares born. Dark wrap that looks upon all things' doom, Reaper's Cloak!"

"No!" She shrieked and lunged, thrusting the blade at him.

The bright weapon shattered when it struck the billowing darkness that settled around him.

Conryu scrambled up, reached back, and pulled the cowl into place. When he did the world turned black and white save for little blue flames just above everyone's navel.

"You see their souls," said the cold voice of the Reaper.

The spy chanted and hurled a bolt of lightning at him. He didn't even feel it when the spell fizzled against his protection.

"All their souls are yours for the taking," the voice of Death said.

Conryu found his gaze drawn to the blue glow in the spy's torso. The knowledge of how to snuff it out appeared in his mind. He need only reach out with his mind and speak the Reaper's true name.

It would be so easy. She'd tried to kill him once already. Her friends had tried it on a regular basis. It would be justified self-defense.

A second lightning bolt, stronger than the first, crackled in before fizzling. The spy's arrogant sneer had turned to a tremble of fear.

"Take her," the cold voice said. "Send her to me and I promise I'll give her an eternity of torment. It's no less than she deserves."

It *was* no less than she deserved, but it wasn't for him to decide. The woman, whoever she was, posed no threat to him. He hadn't killed Mercia when she was at his mercy and he wouldn't kill this one either.

Conryu darted in and hit her in the gut with an uppercut. Some magical protection broke when he struck it, but it didn't slow his blow.

The air rushed out of her and she doubled over. He stepped back and delivered an ax kick to the back of her head, dropping her to the floor and knocking her cold.

A quick scan of the room revealed no other threat. He willed the spell to end, but the magic lingered.

"Eventually you will have to use my power, boy. You won't be able to resist forever. If you won't kill for yourself, then you'll do it for someone else. I have all the time in the universe and once you use it the first time, the second becomes oh so easy."

The cloak vanished in a burst of chill black mist. He sighed in relief when the Reaper's presence disappeared. Prime flew over and hovered beside him. "Are you alright, Master?"

"Yeah." Conryu was surprised to find he meant it.

He was surrounded by unconscious, but unharmed, people. It appeared this business was settled and he was free to return to what passed for his normal life. All in all not a bad result.

Chapter 13

The End

Conryu stared at the Kincade mansion as the limo pulled up beside the front steps. It was bathed in orange light from the sunset. He'd never imagined visiting a place like this. It was the sort of home you saw on tv, not the sort of place someone like him got invited to for dinner. He had to remind himself that no matter how nice the exterior, the inside was rotten.

After everyone recovered from the spy's surprise attack, the president's security detail had hustled him out of the room and for all Conryu knew out of the building. It probably wasn't going to look good on their resume that their charge had been rescued by a teenager. Well, at least he didn't end up having to give the speech. That was a small consolation.

He'd been forced to hang around the Department building while Malice dealt with the fallout from the failed attack. She'd barked orders and waved people here and there for hours. No one had offered him so much as a bottle of water, much less lunch.

The limo stopped and the driver opened the door for them. Conryu climbed out followed by Kelsie and Malice.

Prime flew up beside him. "This place has impressive protections."

"Indeed." Malice started up the steps. "Every generation adds a new layer to the wards. After all these years I doubt even you could break them."

Conryu raised an eyebrow. "Is that a challenge?"

Malice glanced back. "An observation. Please refrain from attempting to dispel our wards. If by some miracle you should succeed it would be inconvenient for me."

She continued up the steps and Conryu looked at Kelsie and rolled his eyes. She smiled and stifled a laugh. It was good to find her smiling again. She'd been pretty shaken up by the attack.

At the top of the stairs the doors opened of their own accord. An old man in a servant's uniform bowed to Malice. "Welcome home, madam. Lady Kincade is waiting for you in the lounge. Dinner will be served in half an hour."

Malice nodded, barely looking at the servant. Conryu had never dealt with a servant before so he just smiled and followed Malice deeper into the mansion. Art covered the walls, but the paintings were the ugliest he'd ever seen. They looked like nothing but random blobs of color.

After a short hike they came to a room filled with soft leather chairs, a chess board on a hardwood table, and a full bar. The lounge was bigger than his whole apartment.

Seated in one of the chairs was a woman that looked exactly like an older version of Kelsie. She wore a black dress slit to her navel, revealing a stunning amount of cleavage. Kelsie let out a soft gasp and Conryu knew just how she felt. Only the strictest mental discipline had kept him from having that same reaction with each new room they entered. Seeing a woman he knew had to be the same age as his mother if not older in such an outfit stunned him. It helped that she looked about thirty.

Kelsie's mother stood up and smiled, revealing teeth too flawless and white to be natural. Not that his gaze lingered long on her teeth, what with all the jiggling going on down below. There had to be some sort of magic holding her dress up.

"You must be Conryu. Kelsie's told me all about you. My name is Cassandra Kincade and I can't thank you enough for helping my daughter with her studies. I'm sure without you she would have failed long ago." She held out her hand and Conryu gave it a polite shake.

"I don't think you give Kelsie enough credit. She works as hard as anyone and harder than many. She's a good friend and I couldn't have accomplished most of what I have without her."

Kelsie's frown had grown into a bright smile just as he'd hoped it would.

Cassandra shook her head causing yet more jiggling. "You're very generous. Would you like a drink?"

"I'm still underage, but thank you."

"Polite and powerful, what an unusual combination." She walked to the bar, working her hips as she went. What in heaven's name was she playing at? Cassandra poured herself a drink and turned to Malice. "Would you like one, Mother?"

"Make it a double. After today, I need it."

Cassandra filled a tumbler three-quarters of the way up with amber liquid and handed it to Malice, being sure to lean over more than she had to so he could get a good look.

Conryu glanced at Kelsie whose face was bright red. If his mother had acted like that Conryu would have been embarrassed as well.

He couldn't begin to describe his relief when the servant opened the door and announced, "Dinner is served."

* * *

Conryu pushed away from a table long enough to seat sixty and sighed. He'd never eaten a meal—no, make that a feast—like that in his life. Eight courses from salad to a little fruit tart for dessert. Beside him Kelsie had only picked at her food. Eating like this all the time probably made you jaded.

He took a sip of water and fought back a yawn. It had been a long day and he was ready to find out if the beds in this place were as comfortable as he imagined.

"Was the meal to your liking?" Cassandra asked.

"It was delicious, thank you." He kept waiting for the other shoe to drop. From Kelsie's description he wouldn't have thought her mother would be this nice.

"Wonderful. Would you join me in my office? I have a business proposition for you."

Here it comes. Still, he couldn't simply refuse the woman in her own house after she provided him with an outstanding meal. "Alright."

Kelsie tugged his sleeve and gave him a concerned look. He offered a weak smile and shrug. Whatever she wanted, Conryu doubted he'd be interested, but it couldn't hurt to hear her out, for Kelsie's sake if nothing else.

He followed Cassandra out of the dining room. As he walked he felt the gaze of both Malice and Kelsie on his back.

Prime flew along beside him, but the scholomantic remained silent. They walked down a long hall decorated like the rest of the house before stopping in front of a closed door.

Cassandra spoke a soft word that he couldn't make out and the door swung open revealing a well-appointed office. She walked across to her desk, turned to face him, and sat on the edge. "I'm not going to mince words with you. I want your genetics added to our bloodline. What's your price?"

"Price?" Though he was pretty sure what she was suggesting Conryu was having trouble fully processing it.

"To impregnate me. I've performed the necessary rituals to ensure my fertility and the survival of any offspring. You'll be in no way responsible for the child or children resulting. When we've agreed on a price I'll draw up a contract stipulating that. It will be necessary for you to remain our guest until pregnancy is confirmed. Even with magical assistance the seed doesn't always take on the first try."

He could only stare as she wrapped up her pitch. And that's what it was, an emotionless transaction. She didn't care about him or her future kid. Improving her bloodline was really all that interested her.

"I'm going to have to pass. Not that I'm not flattered, but I don't think I could do what you want."

"Ten million."

He nearly choked. Ten million to knock her up? That was insane. Not that they couldn't afford it, but still.

"What about Kelsie?"

Her lips turned down in a slight frown. "What about her?"

"I thought she was your heir and that you wanted her to seduce me into—how did you put it, improving your bloodline?"

"She's had half a year. Clearly my daughter isn't up to the task." Cassandra gave a disgusted shake of her head. "She so seldom lives up to my expectations I no longer know why I bother to ask anything of her. Though by attaching herself to you she has improved her status in the world as one of the primary saviors of Sentinel City. That alone will fend off any challenges from within the family. However she's simply too weak to trust with the clan's future."

"Kelsie isn't weak or a failure of any sort. The idea of placing any child, much less my own, in your care, horrifies me." Conryu turned toward the door. "I'll accept your hospitality for tonight and be on my way tomorrow. Hopefully we'll never see each other again."

Master, she's preparing a spell. Prime's voice appeared in his mind.

"Cloak of Darkness!"

Dark magic settled around him an instant before a spell fizzled against it.

He spun. An aura of light magic still surrounded Cassandra's hands. She glared at him. "I will have your power, one way or another."

"That right?" He raised his hand, crossed his fingers, and focused on the magic she'd cast on herself. "Break!"

The black sphere slammed into her chest. Magic crackled and broke apart. Wrinkles appeared on her once-smooth face. Her hair turned gray and her breasts sagged, though they mercifully failed to escape her dress.

She held up her wrinkled hands and stared at them then at him. "What have you done?"

"Not done, undone. I've stripped away all your magic. Stay away from me or I'll bring this house down around your head." He turned on his heel and stalked out.

Prime fell in beside him. "That was close, Master."

"Yeah, thanks for the warning." He let the Cloak of Darkness fade away.

"Protecting you is my job. What will you do now?"

"I'm not sure. Part of me thinks I should leave right now, but it's late and I don't want another fight if I can help it. Do you know any wards that I can use to protect myself if I stay the night?"

"Several, Master, have no fear."

They reached the dining room and found Kelsie pacing and Malice sipping another drink.

"That was fast," the old woman said. "I figured someone your age would have more stamina."

"For the record, I'm not for sale." He turned to Kelsie. "Could you show me to my room? I'm beat."

"Of course." She started for the door.

"Wait." Malice stood up and Conryu prepared himself for a second fight. "How much did you turn down?"

"Ten million. She didn't like that very well and tried using magic on me. Mind control of some sort I believe. She was too slow."

He followed Kelsie out of the room, down a hall, then up a set of stairs. They stopped in front of an open door that led to a large bedroom.

"I'm sorry my mother tried to use you like that. I had no idea she'd go so far." She hugged him.

"It's not your fault. I'm leaving tomorrow. If you want to come back with me you're welcome. This is no place for you, for anybody as far as that goes."

"I will, thank you."

He nodded and went inside the opulent guest room. Before he even thought about sleeping he had to figure out how to ward the room.

* * *

Conryu floated in darkness. He had to be dreaming as he hadn't cast a portal. He tried to orient himself, but there was nothing, no sign of Cerberus either. Yes, it was definitely a dream. When slender arms wrapped themselves around him from behind and warm, soft lips kissed the nape of his neck he spun, ready for a fight.

"Hardly the greeting I expected, Master." The Dark Lady floated a foot away smiling and gorgeous in her black dress.

He relaxed. "Sorry. I expected someone else. How are things in Hell?"

"Better since our contract. No one mocks me now."

"Good. I'm glad to see you. I wasn't sure how to contact you and I wanted to say thanks. Our connection allowed me to successfully dominate a demon and send her back to Hell. I'm sure I couldn't have done it without your extra power."

"Rennet, yes, I know all about that. In fact, she's what brings me here tonight."

Conryu cocked his head. "How so?"

"She contacted me and said the leader of the Le Fay Society wishes to talk to you."

"When?"

"Right now."

"Sounds like a trap." Conryu couldn't imagine what they'd have to talk about in the first place.

"No, Master. She selected this place since you'd be protected by the many wards around Kincade Manor. As long as you don't move beyond the steps you'll be safe. She won't be able to reach you."

"What does she want?"

"I have no idea. Rennet was simply delivering a message." The Dark Lady's lips curled in a cruel smile. "After her failure this is what she's been reduced to. It gives me great pleasure to find her so demeaned."

Conryu nodded absently, his mind rushing along as he considered the implications of this invitation. "What do you think I should do?"

She shrugged. "If there was ever a time to size up your enemy, this is it. It can't do you any harm."

"I guess you're right. Thanks for bringing me the message."

Her expression softened. "My pleasure."

He blinked and sat up in bed. "Prime."

"I heard, Master. I agree with the lady, this is a good chance to see what we're dealing with."

"Right." He slipped out of bed and threw on his clothes.

Now he just had to find his way to the front door without getting lost or running into the crazy people that lived here. He deactivated the dark magic ward he'd set around his bedroom and stepped out into the hall. The house was silent. A hint of moonlight filtered in from somewhere. It wasn't much, but he'd manage.

With Prime flying along at his side Conryu tiptoed through the silent halls, eventually reaching the entry hall. He unlocked the front door and stepped out into the cool night air. Ten feet from the foot of the stairs was a dark figure in a mask.

Conryu marched down and paused on the final step. “You wanted to talk?”

She moved closer revealing the details of her green dragon mask and crimson robe. She looked like a performer at one of the Imperial New Year celebrations. All they were lacking was fireworks.

“I am Lady Dragon, temporary leader of the Society. You have done us a great deal of harm in a year.” She had a warm, pleasant voice, totally different than what he’d expected.

He shrugged. “You all tried to kill me more than once. I can hardly be faulted for fighting back.”

“True. I admit it never crossed my mind that we’d have such difficulty dealing with an inexperienced wizard. Of course, having never encountered a male wizard before, our ignorance is unsurprising.”

“So what happens now?”

“Now? Nothing. But we will see each other again.” Lady Dragon chanted and stepped back into a portal.

Conryu turned to Prime. “That wasn’t encouraging. I was hoping she’d say ‘sorry, let’s let bygones be bygones’ or ‘live and let live,’ something like that.”

“That’s far too optimistic, Master. I fear we’ve begun a war and the first battle just ended.”

Sarcasm was clearly lost on the scholomantic. “At least we won. More or less.”

"Indeed. Let us hope the next battle ends equally well."

Conryu sighed and looked out over the dark grounds. A war, huh? How had it come to this? All he'd ever wanted was a nice, quiet life, work at the bike shop, train with his father, maybe marry Maria someday.

Instead he got secret societies, deranged industrialists, and politicians all wanting to use or end his life. One thing was certain. He wouldn't have to worry about being bored.

Author Notes

And so year one ends of Conryu. He came through it alive, though only just. I hope you enjoyed reading about his adventures in the magical world. Things are only going to get more interesting for our hero as we move forward, but I thought it might be nice to let him enjoy the rest of his summer vacation. In book five we're going to head far to the east and meet another unlucky person who's found to have wizard potential. Like Conryu, she only wants to live a normal life. Instead she finds herself rushing across Europe in an attempt to escape those that would make her a slave. I hope you'll join me for the next installment of the Aegis of Merlin series.

Until next time, thanks for reading.

James

About the Author

James E. Wisher is a writer of science fiction and Fantasy novels. He's been writing since high school and reading everything he could get his hands on for as long as he can remember. This is his thirteenth novel.

Made in the USA
Middletown, DE
20 August 2021